Praise for Barbara Delinsky

"Delinsky is an expert at portraying strong women characters."
Booklist

"Delinsky is one of those writers who knows how to introduce characters to her readers in such a way that they become more like old friends than works of fiction."
Flint Journal

"Delinsky is an engaging writer who knows how to interweave several stories about complex relationships and keep her books interesting to the end. Her special talent for description gives the reader almost visual references to the surroundings she creates."
Newark Star Ledger

"Delinsky's prose is spare, controlled and poignant as she evokes the simplicity and joys of small-town life."
Publishers Weekly

"Delinsky steers clear of treacle . . . with simple prose and a deliberate avoidance of happily ever after clichés."
People

"Delinsky delves deeper into the h̲u̲m̲a̲n̲ ̲h̲e̲a̲r̲t̲ ̲a̲n̲d̲ spirit with each new nov̲

"Barbara Delinsky shou̲ of readers."

"Delinsky creates . . . a re̲ beautiful story."
Baton Rouge Advocate

Books by Barbara Delinsky

BARBARA DELINSKY

Gemstone

HarperTorch
An Imprint of HarperCollinsPublishers

An edition of this book was published in 1983 by Dell Publishing Co., Inc. under the pseudonym Bonnie Drake.

HARPERTORCH
An Imprint of HarperCollins*Publishers*
10 East 53rd Street
New York, New York 10022-5299

First HarperTorch paperback printing: October 2001
First HarperCollins paperback printing: August 1993

HarperCollins ®, HarperTorch™, and ❦™ are trademarks of Harper-Collins Publishers Inc.

Printed in the United States of America

Visit HarperTorch on the World Wide Web at www.harpercollins.com

20 19 18 17 16 15 14

To my son Eric,
with thoughts of a very special time in his life

One

Her hands trembling, Sara McCray slowly flattened the newspaper onto her desk and reread the obituary before her. Alex and Diane Owens? *Alex and Diane dead*? How could it be?

Her brown eyes clouded in her struggle for comprehension. But the printed word wasn't to be denied even upon a third reading. There had been an automobile accident on a slick road just north of San Francisco. Neither passenger had survived the crash.

She sat stunned, shocked into silent mourning for the couple who had been so youthful, so vibrant, so very much in love. They'd been her only friends at a time when it had seemed the world was against her. But she'd left San Francisco eight years ago. She had neither seen them since nor had the opportunity to thank them for their support. The break had been complete . . . as Geoffrey must have wished it.

Geoffrey. The passage of eight years' time had done nothing to stem the involuntary quickening she still felt at the mention of his name. With an unsteady breath she stood and moved toward the window where the night lights of New York glittered against her own slender reflection.

She'd changed. No longer was she that naive young woman he'd found in Colorado ten years before. The image that met her eyes confirmed it.

Then she'd worn simpler clothes, mostly jeans, sweaters and boots. Now she wore fine-tailored wool slacks, a silk blouse and imported leather pumps. Then her blond hair had flowed in free fall down her back. Now it was loosely twisted and chicly caught up with a comb above one ear. Then the crisp Rocky Mountain air had given her cheeks all the blush they'd needed. Now she was delicately made up to counter the pallor of a city dweller.

Shifting, her gaze moved beyond to focus blindly on the night. Yes, she'd changed. But the memories remained. There were memories of Geoffrey . . . of his family . . . of Alex and Diane . . .

Disbelieving still, Sara whirled back to the desk to study the blur of two-day-old newsprint. The words were as clear as ever, their meaning as incredibly grievous despite her reluctance to accept them. She would have liked to see Alex and Diane again, to tell them of all she'd been doing, to thank them for their support way back then. But it was too late . . . too late. Now there were only final respects to be paid.

Her head bowed, she entered the small chapel and slid into an aisle seat in back just as the service was about to begin. The stylish suede hat that dipped low over her eyes hid not only her fatigue from the red-eye flight but the sorrow that had brought her so suddenly west. As for the trepidation she felt, she could only fold her hands in her lap to still their shakiness. It was the first time she'd been back to San Francisco since she and Geoffrey had divorced.

The haunting lilt of the organ tapered off, finally yielding to the minister's low voice. "The Lord is my shepherd . . ."

Raising her eyes for the first time, Sara looked past rows of mourners toward the front of the chapel and the two brass-edged coffins that stood in stark evidence of tragedy. Alex and Diane. So caring. So giving. So understanding. What had they done to deserve such untimely deaths?

She recalled the first time she'd met them, just hours before they'd stood as witnesses to her marriage to Geoffrey. From the start they'd treated her with warmth and acceptance, toasting her future with Jeff, bolstering her during that private flight back to San Francisco, giving her what encouragement they could in preparation for her inevitable confrontation with the Parker world.

It hadn't been nearly enough. *Nothing* could have prepared her for that confrontation, a scene neither to be forgotten nor, she'd vowed at the time of the divorce, repeated.

Suppressing a shudder, she let her attention be drawn back to the minister, whose gentle voice had completed a selection of inspirational readings and embarked on an emotion-laden eulogy for the couple he'd known and admired. Sara listened intently, seeking justification in his words for what had happened to Alex and Diane. *Was* it God's will?

When the achingly sweet strains of "Coming Home" filled the chapel, her eyes brimmed with unexpected tears. Lowering her head, she felt first one, then another, trickle slowly down her cheeks. Her gloved hand drew a handkerchief from her purse and pressed it to her lips.

Yes, there was her sorrow at the passing of two friends. But there was more, far more, that the soulful mood of the music inspired. She felt suddenly and overwhelmingly lonely, as she hadn't felt in years. Was it this city, as opposed to New York which held her life, her career, her friends and co-workers? Was it the memory of what she had once hoped for here—love, family, the warmth of a home filled with children? Or was it the fear that life was short, too short?

The music ended without having supplied the answers to her questions. Yet there was strength in the minister's final words, enough for her to gather her composure and stand with the others while the pallbearers slowly started down the narrow aisle.

She followed their progress intently, her heart beating faster with their approach. Her eye glanced along the first coffin and on to the second. Her fingers clutched at the wooden pew before her. It was inevitable. She'd known it from the moment she'd so hastily decided to attend the funeral. Geoffrey would be here. It would be the first time she'd seen him in eight years.

The pallbearers moved past, then the small group of relatives. Sara's attention barely skimmed them, searching the faces beyond, always beyond. Then she felt a jolt of recognition and caught her breath. There—shoulders weighted beneath a burden of sorrow . . .

He moved slowly, as though each step brought him closer to a future he didn't want to face. Sara couldn't take her eyes from him—his tall, lean frame garbed in a dark suit whose black tie spoke publicly of his mourning, his dark head bowed. Closer he came, closer, until he neared that last pew.

She'd never know what caught his attention: whether it was the power of her own concentration, some other mystical force or simply his arrival at the back of the chapel. But just as he came upon the row in which she stood, he paused, waited, angled his head the barest inch to note her gloved hands gripping the wood. Then slowly, almost fearfully, he raised his eyes.

In that instant her being was suspended in time over an eight-year span. When she'd last seen Geoffrey, he'd been hard and angry. He'd allowed for no hint of sympathy or sorrow, either one of which would easily have stayed her departure.

Now sorrow permeated his being—sorrow and disbelief, even a vulnerability she would never have attributed to a Parker. It was all she could do to keep from reaching out to him. But it wasn't her place . . . not any longer.

His lips moved in a nearly imperceptibly mouthed "Sara?" She bit her lower lip and nodded as faintly, realizing with a start that he might not immediately have recognized her, subsequently wondering whether he'd be angry that she'd presumed to intrude on what had to be such a personal tragedy for him. The last thing she'd wanted was to make things worse.

But rather than anger she saw confusion, disorientation, wavering—feelings that became her own when his eyes softened in a silent plea and his hand moved tentatively toward hers. In the instant's hesitation she understood that despite what had happened in the past, today she shared a small part of his sorrow. And if Geoffrey sought her solace, she needed his as well. Without further thought she slipped her hand into his and let him draw her to his side to resume the walk from the chapel.

The late fall air was crisp, the brightness of the sun seeming ineffective, even inappropriate. Geoffrey held her hand close to his thigh, his long fingers locked tightly around her more slender gloved hand. He looked forward, as did she. Neither spoke. When they reached the car that stood waiting by the curb, Sara slid in across the backseat. He followed her quickly, not releasing her hand once.

The car inched forward and fell into line to wait while those behind took on passengers. It struck Sara that had she not been here, Geoffrey would have been alone. Alone. It seemed totally out of character. While they'd been married, he'd thrived on that endless succession of social engagements that had sent her into a tailspin of nervous tension.

Having followed the San Francisco newspapers faithfully, she knew that he hadn't remarried. Somehow, though, she'd always pictured him surrounded by people. President of Parkington Enterprises, trustee of numerous educational and charitable institutions, respected member of the country club, the men's club, high society itself ... .

Daring a glance up at him now, she found it

hard to believe this preoccupied man to be the same one whose life she'd followed over the years. Oh, he was as darkly handsome, as compelling in his way. But he was distracted, brooding. She might even have thought him oblivious to her presence, had it not been for the hand that gripped hers as though it were the only stable base in a world of flux.

As if reading her thoughts, he shifted his gaze to study the intertwining of their fingers. Then, to her bemusement, he relaxed his grip enough to remove her glove and resume the clasp flesh to flesh. Given the somber cause for their reunion, Sara could almost understand his desire for this living warmth. Almost . . . but not quite. For, among other things, the man she'd married had been an icon of self-containment. He'd never truly *needed* her as, ironically, he seemed to at this moment.

Holding her hand snug atop his thigh, he gently moved his thumb back and forth over her softer skin. Quite against her will, she found pleasure in the gesture. But then, she reminded herself, she'd always found pleasure in his touch. That much hadn't changed. That much would *never* change.

The air in the car seemed suddenly that much closer. Sara held her breath, not knowing what else to do. When Geoffrey slid his thumb up and around the polished oval of one fingernail, she recalled that he'd never seen her hands in this state of refinement. He, too, seemed to ponder the change, frowning in confusion at this small but telling difference. Then, slowly, he looked upward.

Meeting his gaze, Sara's heart went out to him. The man she'd known years ago had been sure of himself and his direction. This man, mere inches from her now, seemed lost and lonely, tormented by sorrow as she'd *never* imagined him to be.

What *had* she imagined when she'd rushed to book the first flight out of New York last night? She'd imagined attending the funeral, paying her last respects to a couple she'd never forget, perhaps nodding to Geoffrey in passing; that was all. She would never have imagined finding herself alone with him, much less offering him a kind of solace. The extent of his distraction was something she couldn't fathom. He'd certainly let *her* go easily enough.

The slow movement of the car was enough to scatter the germ of bitterness that had no place in the current scheme of things. She was a different woman now than she'd been then.

And she was here simply to give a sadly belated thanks to two people who'd been kind to her. That was all. Seeing Geoffrey again was irrelevant.

But irrelevancy was one thing, curiosity quite another. When the car picked up speed and he turned to impose his anguished stare on the passing scenery, Sara took advantage of his distraction to silently reacquaint herself with the profile she'd once known so well. It was Geoffrey indeed, from the deep set of his steel-gray eyes down the aristocratic line of his nose to a pair of firm lips and a squared-off jaw.

He'd aged. Eight years had a way of doing that. In Geoffrey's case there were ghosts of laugh lines by his eyes and his mouth; newer, more somber grooves on his brow and beneath his eyes. He was obviously tired, and in great psychological pain.

The pain only increased upon their arrival at the cemetery, where the aura of heartbreaking finality added to the elemental chill. Geoffrey was a tall, dark form beside her, deliberately holding himself straight. Yet the crushing pressure of his hand around hers belied his outer control, and quite helplessly Sara found herself drawn into his grief. Tears welled in her eyes, rendering them limpid brown pools that reflected the pain of a host of lost chances. Life was short . . . and dear. The realization of its fragility shook her deeply.

With the last of the prayers intoned, the minister closed his book and moved slowly through the group of mourners. Sara stood at Geoffrey's side, her head bowed both in sorrow and respect. She was the intruder here. Had Geoffrey not gripped her hand so convulsively, she would have stepped far to the side to allow him the privacy of the quiet condolences that were offered. One by one the other mourners approached, some murmuring gentle words, others simply squeezing his arm. When she finally dared raise her eyes, they were the only two left.

Then, for the first time since he'd seen her in the chapel, he let her hand fall free. Walking slowly forward, he stopped before the matching coffins, reaching out first to one, then the other in a futile, tender gesture. Sara read the intense grief on his face and, feeling once more the trespasser, turned to leave. She hadn't taken a full two steps when his voice stayed her.

"Sara . . . ?"

She waited, frozen in place, unsure of what to do. By rights, having paid her final respects to Alex and Diane, it was time to head back to the airport. There'd been meetings canceled, appointments hastily postponed. New York awaited her.

But something in his tone arrested her, something she'd ached to hear eight years ago and hadn't. She simply couldn't move.

"Sara?" Edged with desolation, his voice came from directly behind her. "Come back to the house with me."

When she looked back up at him, he slipped his hand in hers. Only then did she realize how cold her fingers had been without his touch.

He didn't wait for her answer. With one long, last glance back at his friends, he bent his head and started for the car. It was a different car this time, no longer the formal funeral limousine. This one was sleek and gray, with license plates identifying a vehicle of Parkington Enterprises, *RPE-1*. While Sara had been a Parker, Cecelia Parker's car had always borne these plates. Indeed, the chauffeur who opened the door had been Cecelia Parker's driver as well.

As recognition hit Sara, she wondered if it would be mutual. The house staff had frowned on her nearly as much as had Geoffrey's mother. But the man's gaze didn't flicker. He nodded politely, innocently, before looking at Geoffrey for direction.

"We'll be going home, Cyrus," he murmured softly.

"Certainly, Mr. Parker."

Home. The word echoed in Sara's mind as she slid into the car once more. Geoffrey followed her smoothly, then took her hand into his lap and stared at it broodingly.

Home. The magnificent mansion in which she'd suffered so. For an instant she wondered why she'd ever agreed to this folly. Then she cast a glance up at Geoffrey and knew. She hadn't had the heart to argue. He was so obviously distraught at the deaths of his closest friends that if the simple fact of her presence could comfort him, for old times' sake so be it.

In the silence that dominated the drive toward the southerly suburbs of San Francisco, Sara grew uneasy. For with the increasing familiarity of the roads came a corresponding flow of memory. Much as she tried to stem it, to concentrate on the present, it seemed an impossible task.

Once more she was the starry-eyed innocent who'd arrived as Geoffrey's new bride ten years before. There were the same goose bumps when the car passed through the gates of the Parker estate and purred beneath a lavish evergreen canopy up the long, winding drive. There was the same surge of awe when the stately home came into view, the same sense of anticipation when the car came to a halt beneath the broad portico, the same wave of apprehension when Geoffrey helped her out and led her to the same front door that opened right on cue. For a split second she held her breath, awaiting the same onrush of shocked Parkers.

But there was no onrush. The mood was somber and quiet. Aside from the maid who'd opened the door, there wasn't a soul in sight. The stark contrast of memory with reality brought Sara quickly to the present.

She didn't recognize the maid, and Geoffrey didn't pause to make introductions. Rather he nodded perfunctorily and moved directly through the large front hall to the adjacent library. Once inside, he closed its double doors and crossed to the heavy oak desk, where he stood with his back to her. Sara waited.

After what seemed an eternity of silent deliberation, he squared his shoulders, raised his head and turned. She grew instantly cautious.

But it was unnecessary. There was nothing remotely threatening in his gaze, nothing but a suffusive sadness.

"I think I could use a drink," he began softly. "Would you like one?"

Considering the lack of sleep she'd had the night before, a drink would have done dreadful things. "No . . . thanks." She stood awkwardly while Geoffrey lined the bottom of a snifter with pale amber liquid and downed it in a swallow. Then he put the glass firmly down, raked a hand through his hair and gave himself a minute to absorb the liquor's warmth.

Contrarily, Sara's own disturbance grew. Now that she was here, she had no idea what she was to do. Geoffrey's fierce hold of her hand had given her direction, but now that was gone. Again she waited for his lead.

It came instants later when he cast her a somber glance. "Would you excuse me for a few minutes? There's . . . something I've got to do."

"Sure." She shrugged, nodded, looked behind her at the rich leather sofa.

He followed her line of sight. "Make yourself comfortable. I'll be right back."

Moments later Sara sat quietly ensconced in a protective corner of the sofa, wondering what in the world she was doing here, in this library, in this house. When she'd left eight years before she'd wished never to return.

Then she'd had no idea what she wanted— only that she didn't want any part of either the Parkers or the money they'd offered so bloodlessly. She'd set out simply to earn a living and in the process had truly found herself. She had nothing to fear from the Parkers now, or so the rationalization went as she smoothed the soft wool of her skirt, idly tucked a loose wisp of hair back into its twist, fished in her purse for the pale coral lipstick that would moisten her suddenly dry lips.

She had nothing to fear—but the memories— and no possible way to ward them off now that she sat smack dab at the scene of that long-ago fiasco. In a final bid for diversion she sent an appraising glance around the library. It was a large room, dominated first by that massive oak desk, second by the floor-to-ceiling bookshelves that seemed only grudgingly to allow for the intrusion of the double doors and three tall windows.

As opposed to so many of the other rooms that were redecorated on a regular basis, this one kept its rare atmosphere, a vintage wine aged and mellow. Sara would have liked to spend more time in it during the years of her marriage, had it not been for the fact that it had then been the stronghold of Geoffrey's mother. She'd held court here, served as chairman of the board here. For that matter, it was here that she'd first voiced her disdain for Sara.

Like sharks moving in at the first smell of blood, the memories returned. Sara had been eighteen at the time, freshly graduated from high school, working as a waitress at an exclusive resort in Snowmass. She'd always wanted to learn to ski, she'd reasoned, but money had been too tight; and the wheat fields of Iowa were a far cry from the Colorado Rockies. When the waitressing job—her ticket to the world beyond—had come through, she'd been ecstatic, and she'd been even more so when she'd had her first breathtaking view of the mountains.

She'd begun work with unlimited enthusiasm, determined to live lightly, enjoy herself, save whatever money she could for college one day. It hadn't quite worked out that way. She'd barely been on the job for a month when Geoffrey had arrived for a ski holiday.

He'd instantly caught her eye, despite every warning she'd given herself against mixing with the resort's wealthy guests. As many times as she reminded herself that an unsophisticated young working girl was totally out of league with a man of his social standing, she was helplessly drawn to his dark good looks, his athletic physique, the air of worldliness he possessed so casually.

At the time she'd been unaware of his own equivocation. Only later had he confessed to many of the same thoughts, all of which he'd finally ignored when, two days later, he'd asked her out.

Having read her hesitancy well, he'd been slow and gentle, first simply taking her for a drink after work, spending time talking with her rather than barreling her into bed as she'd half feared. Somehow they'd managed to find common ground on which their respective backgrounds were irrelevant. And Sara had quickly fallen in love.

As the week had passed they'd spent more and more time together. Whenever Sara was free from work, Geoffrey was there to suggest some new adventure. They talked, played, grew increasingly attracted to one another. It was all so warm and innocent . . . until that last night when, prompted by his scheduled departure the next morning their mutual restraint crumbled.

With a tingle of remembered rapture, Sara wrapped her arms around her middle. It had been beautiful, positively beautiful. He'd been a gentle lover, a masterful one. The loss of her virginity had been a small price compared to that huge chunk of her heart he'd seized.

When, with the break of morning, he'd proposed marriage, she'd accepted without hesitation. She loved him; he loved her. The differences between them were nothing, *nothing*, in the face of their love.

Unfortunately, Cecelia Parker was nowhere near as blissful when, after a stop in Reno, they arrived as man and wife in San Francisco that evening. As the scene unfolded in living color on the video screen of her memory, Sara shuddered.

Cecelia Parker had been livid. "You're *what?*"

"Married, Mother. Sara and I were married this afternoon." Geoffrey had stood tall, holding Sara close to make his point. But his mother had refused at first even to recognize her presence.

"Who *is* she?" she'd asked in a tone clear and insulting enough to have stung Sara to the quick. Geoffrey had tried to prepare her for the inevitable resistance, as had Alex and Diane.

But outright rudeness was something that Sara, lowly social status notwithstanding, knew enough to avoid. Not so Mrs. Parker.

"Who *is* she?" she'd repeated when Geoffrey had looked at Sara to try silently to ease her hurt.

"Her name is—"

"You've already told me her name. Who *is* she?"

"She's my wife," he'd replied with deadly calm, refusing to be intimidated.

But he'd learned his technique from his mother. She was the expert. Even now, ten years later, Sara could remember the studied poise of her—the sleekly bound knot of her thick silver hair, the impeccable fall of her designer suit, the polished tips of her foreign-made heels. And her face . . . her face had worn a mask of utter composure betrayed only by the fire in her eyes and the venom on her tongue.

"That much I've heard," she'd replied grimly. "But where does she come from? Where did you meet her? Who are her parents?"

Reliving that humiliating ordeal, Sara rose from the sofa, paced to a window, finally decided that a drop of brandy might do the trick after all.

Where had she come from? She'd come from Iowa, the fifth of six children. Where had he met her? She'd been waitressing at the ski resort at which he'd been a high-paying guest. Who were her parents? Her parents had been struggling farm workers, with nothing to give their children but love.

Geoffrey had been less blunt, of course, though he'd known every fact from the start. He'd tried to smooth over the rough edges, placing emphasis on the positive things that he and Sara had discovered in each other. Even to her own ears, though, the discrepancies in their backgrounds were appalling. And Cecelia Parker made a point of systematically emphasizing each and every one. Love, in her book, was irrelevant.

Despite Geoffrey's support, despite his repeated vows of love, things had gone downhill from there. As many times as he stood up to his mother in Sara's favor, Mrs. Parker had shrewdly analyzed her opponent and arrived at a well-calculated plan. There were no heated accusations regarding the haste of the marriage, no indignant charges that Sara had played on her innocence to force Geoffrey into marriage. There were neither irate demands for an annulment nor angry threats against

Geoffrey's position in the corporation. Cecelia Parker was far too artful for that. Rather she set out to prove conclusively to her son that Sara was an unfit wife.

It had been a steadily darkening nightmare for Sara, with her mother-in-law as the sinister force behind one social failure after another. Nothing in Sara's background had prepared her for sudden propulsion into high society. She had no knowledge of how to dress, how to drink, how to carry on idle cocktail chatter, much less how to hostess biweekly dinner parties for twelve or more.

With the passing of the months, she'd begun to dread the days and weeks spent with Geoffrey's friends. She'd felt gauche and out of place, finally resorting to making excuses whenever possible. Try as he might, Geoffrey had been unable to understand.

It had been her own fault, she'd later decided. She'd been far too young to understand that her insecurity had been an even greater enemy than her mother-in-law. When she should have talked with Geoffrey, she'd kept things inside. The honesty that had played such an important part in their whirlwind courtship fell prey to a defensiveness that slowly, week after week, month after month, broadened the rift between them. In the end, after two increasingly unhappy years, Sara had simply given up. And Geoffrey had let her go.

"I'm sorry."

A deep voice broke into her sad reverie, bringing her head up with a start. It took her several seconds to understand the meaning of his apology. He stood at the door, having just returned from whatever had kept him so long. And he was certainly not apologizing for having let her go eight years ago!

"No, no," she said softly. "Don't apologize. I was just . . . gathering my thoughts." It was, in its way, the truth.

"I see you've helped yourself to a drink."

She suspected he'd seen much more in those few unguarded seconds before she'd realized he'd returned, but she refused to look away in guilt. "I've been going straight since yesterday morning. If I pass out on the sofa, you'll understand."

He looked better—still tired, but somehow more relaxed. And he actually smiled. For the first time she caught a glimpse of the man whose face had lit up so often for her when they'd first met. From the start that small dimple in his right cheek had done disturbing things to her. Even now her pulse quickened. No, she mused, some things *would* never change.

"It wouldn't be the first time," he teased her gently, seeming to take reassurance from the blush that stole to her cheeks. "But Mrs. Fleming should have lunch ready. That would help."

"Oh, Geoffrey. I don't know." She sat straighter and pushed back the cuff of her blouse to eye her watch. "I really should be going. I was hoping to take an afternoon flight back to New York." She hadn't planned on any diversion, least of all this one. She'd simply wanted to attend the funeral.

"You mean to say that you flew all this distance only to spend a few hours here?" His deep voice registered outright surprise, but it was the faintest note of skepticism in his voice to which she responded.

"It was a last-minute decision. I wanted to . . . do something for Alex and Diane. They were kind to me."

The enigmatic cast of Geoffrey's gaze was lost to her when he looked down. He hadn't moved from the door but stood before it with both hands tucked deep in his pockets. She'd seen that stance only once before, on the day she'd been waiting with her bags packed when he'd returned home from work. At the time she'd interpreted it as a pose of indignation. Now it conveyed a helplessness she attributed to her mention of the day's sad occasion.

His voice was lower, his gaze more direct when he looked back up at her. "Do you always beat yourself into the ground these days? I can remember you loving leisure."

"That," she replied as softly, "was in Colorado, before I discovered how tedious a steady diet of it can be." It was a not-so-subtle slam at the ways of the idle rich, but she went quickly on. "My life is very busy now."

"You look pale. You used to be so tan all the time—"

"I was different in many ways back then. It's been a long time, Jeff."

At the truth of her words, he frowned. She watched a fleeting shadow cross his features and wondered whether he'd ever regretted their divorce. Over the years he'd never tried to contact her or see her. Wasn't he the slightest bit curious as to what she'd become?

A deep sigh broadened his chest. "Eight years," he breathed, then paused. "You've been busy."

So he did know something. "Yes. As I'm sure you have."

When he nodded a swathe of dark hair fell lower on his brow to cover the worry lines she'd seen there. He looked suddenly younger, so very much like the man she'd married that she swallowed hard against the rise of emotion. Strange, that the memory of her love for him could survive that of the hurt she'd suffered.

"Please, Sara," he began as if her thoughts were shared, "stay and have lunch with me. If you want to leave later, I'll drive you to the airport."

"I *have* to leave later," she spoke for herself as for his information. "I've got appointments scheduled in my office from eight tomorrow morning on."

Mention of her work brought a tightening to his jaw. So like his mother, she mused. Calm, collected . . . betrayed only by the look of an eye, the faint working of a muscle.

"Then why don't we go into the other room." Opening the door behind him, he offered her a hand in invitation.

It was that hand, whose warmth had soothed her earlier, that decided the matter. Her own went to it quite willingly, and she let it draw her from the sofa. After all, she needed to eat at some point. And then there was the matter of her own curiosity.

Many changes had taken place in her life over the course of the years; his had changed as well. The marked silence in this home, which years before had been a steady hub of activity, attested to that. Sara had been prepared for Cecelia's absence. But what had become of the rest of the Parker clan—Geoffrey's younger brother and sister, the aunt and uncle who'd lived in the west wing? And where were the friends who'd seemed always to be here, the staff that had milled constantly. Above all, though, she wondered about Geoffrey. What had *he* become in the years since she'd known him?

At this moment she felt no bitterness. She'd weathered the storm of memory in finer shape than she'd ever expected. Perhaps the brandy had helped, she mused. More likely it had been her own self-confidence that had seen her through.

She *was* a different woman from the one who'd left Geoffrey in defeat eight years before. There were no jellied knees, no sweaty palms such as had always before besieged her in this room. She was composed and in full control, ironically more of a Parker now than she'd ever been then.

In some ways she was grateful. Had her marriage not fallen so dismally apart, she might always have followed in Geoffrey's wake—even worse, in that of his mother. Now, though, she was a success in her own right. And it was from this position of strength that she yielded to curiosity.

"Shall we?" she suggested softly, ignoring Geoffrey's sudden bewilderment to smile gently up at him. In the end it was she who took the first step.

Two

In the time it took them to move from the library through the foyer and down the hall past the larger dining hall to the less formal breakfast room, Geoffrey resumed control. He'd been thrown just now, much as he'd been thrown the instant he'd seen Sara in the chapel this morning. In the oppression of the past few days, he'd never stopped to consider that she might come to the funeral.

He was still surprised. To his knowledge she'd never been anywhere near San Francisco since the divorce. It had to have been a difficult decision for her to make, knowing that so many of her memories would be unpleasant ones. Yet she'd come.

Now, holding her chair, he watched her slip into it with a grace she'd never had before. She'd been awkward with formalities then, seeming to resent a way of life that imposed inhibitions in exchange for privilege. *Tamed?* Was that the word to describe her? Or was it simply . . . *matured?*

Taking his own seat to her right, he sat back and studied her. *Matured;* perhaps that was it. He'd had a glimpse in the library of her emotional flux, from the look of near-pain when first he'd reentered the room to her gradual calming and eventual poise. There was an inner strength to her now. If only she'd had it then.

Sara was oblivious to his study, engrossed as she was in a reacquaintance with her surroundings. "I always preferred this room," she mused aloud, "even though we only had breakfast here. It was quieter, more intimate." The room was an oversize octagon connected to the kitchen by a set of french doors. Its walls were of pure glass paned in small segments to disperse the sunlight gaily. In the mornings it had been reassuringly cheerful.

Even now, an hour after noon, it had an airiness that was refreshing.

Geoffrey took intent note of her appreciation. "I eat here all the time now. It's . . . simpler." With the appearance of the same woman who had opened the door when they arrived, he averted his gaze momentarily. "Mrs. Fleming, this is my ex-wife, Sara McCray." The pronouncement brought a wisp of surprise, even pleasure to the woman's eyes, but Geoffrey had already turned back to Sara. "Mrs. Fleming has been with me for two years now. I don't know what I'd have done without her." It was no pat praise; he was fully in earnest.

Sara nodded and exchanged a smile with the spare middle-aged woman whose uniform was a simple skirt and blouse, as opposed to the starched gray Cecelia Parker's staff had worn. She offered a soft thank you when the woman placed a generous slice of melon before her, then waited politely until she was alone with Geoffrey once more.

"She seems pleasant, more human than—than the others."

Geoffrey smiled ruefully. "You never did take to my mother's staff, did you?"

"It was more the other way around," Sara countered, undaunted.

"Perhaps." He gave her the point before sobering. "Either way, they're gone."

Gone. The word ricocheted from one wall to another before Sara could react to its finality. She focused on the gentle curve of the sterling spoon by her plate.

"Jeff," she began softly, "I'm sorry . . . about your mother."

"How could you be? She was wretched to you."

Her gaze swung up. "I'm sorry that you lost her. I know how close you all were."

He shrugged. "There's close . . . and then there's close. My mother was an officious woman who kept an eagle eye on us all. Her death was in many ways a blessing." After a pause he smirked. "I think you can understand. You didn't rush out here for *her* funeral."

"I considered it."

"But . . . ?"

Quietly and honestly she explained her decision. "I felt that, had she known, she would have been offended. She despised me from the start."

Growing more pensive, Geoffrey poked at his melon. "It wasn't really *you* she despised.

How could she? She never got to know you. It was the fact that you were from a different world . . . and the fact that we had dared to defy her by marrying without her consent."

"You were twenty-eight at the time!"

"I know that and you know that," he answered levelly, "but my mother couldn't have cared less. She wanted this house run *her* way or not at all. That's why I said what I did about her death. It's freed all of us."

Which reminded Sara. "Where is everyone, Jeff? You don't really live in this house alone?"

"Yes."

"What about Gordie? And Emily?"

"Gordie just turned thirty. He manages our research division in Palo Alto and has his own place not far from there. As for Emily," he sighed and gazed toward the distant hemlocks in contemplation of his kid sister, "she's off somewhere with her guru. I think it's Paris this month."

"Her guru?" Sara smiled her appreciation. Three years her junior, Emily might have even been her friend had she not been so busy rebelling against everything Sara had been trying so desperately to emulate. "Emily always was a free spirit. I remember the fights *she* had with your mother."

Geoffrey remembered them also, and far too well. "Like fire and water, those two. Emily refused to be fit into the mold."

"And you, Jeff? It didn't bother you?"

He looked at her sharply. "You never asked questions like that when we were married."

"I never thought to," she replied quietly. "When I lived in this house I felt as though I couldn't question *anything*. Your mother was . . . slightly overpowering."

Geoffrey considered her words, knowing that there were any number of other, more bitter ones Sara might have used. Staring at her, he marveled at her equanimity. Then he succumbed to a burst of spontaneity. "Would she overpower you now, if she were still alive?"

There was an intensity, both to his gaze and his question, that took Sara aback for a minute. When she spoke, though, it was with confidence. "No. I don't think so." There was a nearly imperceptible uptilt of her chin even as her voice lowered. "She wouldn't have anything to offer me now that I don't already have." It was a statement of fact, totally devoid of arrogance. Geoffrey sensed as much.

"You've done well, Sara. I wish I could claim even the smallest bit of credit for what you've done since we split, but I can't. You never touched the money, did you?"

She put her spoon down and shook her head. "No. It's still in the bank. You knew I didn't want—"

He held up a hand. "I knew. But there were selfish motives involved. I wanted to be assured that you'd never have to go without." His smile was crooked. "It looks like you've taken care of yourself. At one point you couldn't have afforded the plane fare here from Denver. Now you can pick up and fly cross-country for the sake of a few hours' time." The smile faded and he grew suddenly more grim. "How did you find out about Alex and Diane?"

"I . . . saw it in the newspaper."

"The New York Times?" To his knowledge there'd been no notice placed there.

She shook her head. *"The Chronicle."*

"*Our* paper?" When she nodded, he studied her again. "Why would you be reading it?"

Sara felt suddenly uncomfortable. She'd been receiving the San Francisco paper for years, telling herself that she wanted to keep up with what was happening in the city that had once, albeit briefly, been her home.

"I . . . I periodically consider doing business on the West Coast," she improvised. It was, in fact, an idea that had been promoted by her financial advisers. She had personally vetoed it.

"I see." He glanced up then as Mrs. Fleming appeared at the door and continued only when she'd left behind two large plates of fresh seafood salad. Ignoring the food, he sat back. "Tell me about your business, Sara." His intensity went beyond mere curiosity.

She shrugged off a feeling of unease. "It's not all that earth-shaking. I make jewelry."

"That much I know," he chided more gently. "But tell me how you got started. It's not every day that a one-time waitress becomes a successful designer of jewelry."

"No, I suppose not," she murmured, then went on more pointedly. "But, then, it's not every day that a one-time waitress has an intense two-year encounter with high society. It's amazing what one can pick up, even from the dog house." Her voice had risen; she quickly lowered it and shifted gears. "You knew that I liked to draw."

His eyes were gray and level. "I knew that you used to escape to the solarium when you were upset. It was only after you'd gone that I found a pile of your sketches out there."

"Sketching was an outlet. It relaxed me."

"But the transition from paper sketch to actual jewelry—how did it come about?"

Aside from an occasional sip of water, Sara paid no more heed to the lunch Mrs. Fleming had prepared than did Geoffrey. She eyed him sheepishly. "When one runs out of money in a strange town, one begins to read little signs here and there. In my case the town was Tucson and the sign in the window of the jewelry store said DESIGNS. ONE DOLLAR EACH."

His mien was of deadly quiet. "What were you doing in Tucson?"

They were hitting on touchy ground now, inching closer to that day on which they'd parted. As she projected her thoughts back to that painful time, she felt her veneer of composure begin to slip. It was all she could do to keep her poise.

"I guess you could say I was wandering. I'd left here; I couldn't go back to Iowa."

"Couldn't?"

Feeling chastised against her will, she averted her gaze. But it only caught on the hand resting on the arm of his chair. The softest of dark hairs edged beyond his cuff, the strongest of fingers lay in studied relaxation. She remembered how she'd loved to trace those fingers, how she'd coaxed them into doing such sweet erotic things. Not that it had taken much coaxing in those days. Their bodies had been totally compatible, flagrantly combustible right up to the very end.

Defensively she turned her attention to the white linen napkin on her lap. Then, disgusted that she should be so weak, she eyed him more boldly. "Your family weren't the only ones against our marriage, Jeff. Much as my parents may have wanted to support me, they thought I'd made a terrible mistake. Why do you think they never visited?" she asked, eyes flashing. "It wasn't just the money. Lord knows how many times I offered to send them the air fare. It was *them*. They wouldn't have fit into your world, and they knew it."

His expression grave, Geoffrey sat silently for several moments. "You never told me that."

"There were many things I never told you," she whispered, "but that was half the trouble." With a sad gaze, then a sigh, she returned to the point of departure from her story. "Anyway, I had *my* pride, too. I couldn't very well run back to Des Moines with my tail between my legs. It seemed easier to write them about our separation and tell them that I'd be traveling around for a while."

"Weren't they worried?"

Weren't you? she wondered, then stifled the hurt. "I told them not to be, that you'd seen to my financial security. It wasn't a total lie."

He shot her a punishing glance but passed on a verbal argument. "So it all started in Tucson?"

Sara lifted her fork to idly prod a crisp piece of shrimp. "You really don't want to hear this—"

"I do."

His low, somber tone brooked no argument. Neither did the intensity of the dark gray eyes that pierced her purposefully. She felt the same unease she'd shrugged off earlier, the sense of there being an object to his questioning that went beyond simple sentimentality. In the end she decided she was imagining things, that the tension in him was a product of the strain he'd been under since the Owenses' accident.

"You sold your designs in Tucson?" She nodded. "What kind of designs were they?"

"Oh, mostly earrings at first, then a few bracelets." Pausing, she speared a single green grape and slid it into her mouth. With the fruit's sweetness fresh on her lips, she looked at Geoffrey. "You really should eat. This is very good."

Her words sailed past him unheard. "How could you ever support yourself selling designs here and there for a dollar a shot?"

"It was . . . a challenge." Her lips twitched at the corners in wry recollection. "Let's say that I lived very modestly for a while." There seemed no point in elaborating on the hovel of a room she'd taken, or on the fact of her mercifully light appetite. "I made enough on the designs to buy some supplies—beads and wires and all—to start making my own earrings. When I sold those I had enough to buy finer materials, better tools." She looked at him askance. "Come on, Geoffrey. You know how a business gets going. Use your imagination."

The faintest spark flared in his eye. "I'm trying, princess, but it's mind-boggling to think of translating several one-dollar earring designs into a multimillion-dollar gemstone trade in eight short years."

She would have questioned him on the source of his information had it not been for that one word he'd used with such nonchalance: *Princess.* That was what he'd always called her in their closest moments, an endearment that had been born under a Colorado moon when he'd told her of his world. Princess . . . only in his arms had it been true.

Wiping the stricken look from her face, she cleared her throat. "They, uh, they didn't seem so short living through them. Even now the days are sometimes endless."

He arched a dark brow. "Not endless as in boredom?"

"No. I love my work." Her voice was low and sincere, her eyes soft with pride. "I'd have to love it to put in the seventy-hour weeks I do."

She hadn't really anticipated a response, though she was well accustomed to both surprise and admiration. Geoffrey exhibited neither. To her astonishment, his expression hardened.

"A seventy-hour week doesn't leave much free time. What about *you*, Sara? When do you do the things you want?"

She didn't blink. "I want to make my business a success. Working *is* what I want to do."

"You never wanted to remarry?"

It hadn't been from lack of offers. But she'd never loved another man. And if, even *with* love, she'd failed once . . . "No."

"And you didn't want children."

The first had been a question; this was a statement. Sara stared. "What gave you that idea?" she blurted out, unthinking.

His gaze didn't falter. "You insisted on taking birth-control pills during the entire two years of our marriage, even though you knew how much I wanted children."

Her heart thudded loudly. "You never said it as bluntly as that. For that matter, how could you have thought to have a child with our marriage as shaky as it was?" Her voice lowered to a whisper. "I was little more than a child myself." In so many, many ways.

Awash with guilt, she couldn't tell him that she'd never taken those pills, that she'd thrown them down the drain each night, that she'd never had the courage to tell him that she doubted she could have a child. She'd been young, unsure, unable to believe that he'd love her all the same.

Each lost in his or her own thoughts, they ate in silence for a while. Sara had long since begun simply to shift the food on her plate when Geoffrey stood with a start, tossed his napkin to the table and stalked toward the doorway. He stopped without turning.

"What are your plans now?" His voice came in a rumble from deep within his chest.

She stared at the broad expanse of his shoulders, then put down her fork, sat back and let her gaze fall to her lap. "I've got to get back to New York," she answered quietly.

"And what if you don't?" He turned slowly to eye her cautiously. "What if you were to decide to spend several days here? What if you were sick, or an emergency came up that would keep you from Sara McCray Originals for a while?"

She detected a note of scorn in his voice but refused to be cowed by it. "The business is far from a one-woman operation. It would survive. I've been lucky enough to find good people. They'd easily take care of things."

His gaze narrowed. "But you're the heart of it all?"

"I suppose." She peered at her watch and stood smoothly, sensing that the time had come. "I really should be going. Please thank Mrs. Fleming for lunch. It was lovely. If you could call a cab—"

The thought died on her lips when Geoffrey materialized directly in front of her. On reflex, she tipped up her face. His superior height, his striking build, his darkly intense good looks brought a swell of anticipation to nerve ends that had long lain dormant.

His gaze fell to her lips, tracing their fragility before returning unguardedly to her eyes. "What if I asked you to stay," he began, overlooking her fearful expression, "just until to-

45

morrow? What if I asked you to keep me company—"

But she'd already begun to shake her head. "I can't—"

"Just company. Nothing else."

"Jeff, I—"

Though he spoke with dignity, his expression bore a naked plea. "I don't want to be alone, Sara. Not today."

In the process of lunching with him she'd managed to push the more immediate tragedy from her mind. Now it surged back, blanching her cheeks and wrenching at her heart. In the chapel that morning he'd reached for her. Now she felt that same tug, this time from a spot more deep and private.

"I can't . . ." she whispered, her voice tremulous.

He heard every word she hadn't said, and his tone softened to a caress. "Only what you want—"

"But I can't give you what *you* want," she murmured more urgently. She could feel her resolve weakening, but it was critical he understand.

His palms gently molded to her shoulders. "Time, Sara. One day of your time. That's all I ask."

Had she not been involved in a desperate attempt to slow her racing pulse, she might have reflected more deeply on this turning of the tables. What had been true at the funeral that morning was true again now: Geoffrey needed her. It was a thought far headier than anything she'd ever known. Far headier—and more frightening. "I don't know . . ."

"Please, Sara?"

Filled with anguish, his eyes spoke volumes. He was a human being in pain and in need. Much further, he'd been her husband, the man she'd adored for years. How could she possibly turn her back on him?

In an instinctive gesture of comfort, she raised her hand to his chest, then, catching herself, dropped it. Her gaze fell likewise. With the decision made, she took a deep breath. "I'll have to make several calls . . ."

The release of his tension was a tangible thing, starting in the fingers that held her shoulders and working its way through his long, sinewed length. When she dared to look back up at his face, it was a quiet beacon of gratitude. Then, as though recoiling the strands of emotion that had momentarily and unexpectedly unraveled, he drew back.

"Why don't you use the phone in the library. You can be comfortable there."

She nodded and walked around him, trying her best not to reveal the extent of her unsureness. But that unsureness wasn't as great as when she found herself, moments later, seated at the handsome oak desk, lifting the phone on a matter of business much as Cecelia Parker had done so many times.

Receiver in hand, she darted a glance at the watchful presence that had silently commandeered the doorjamb. Had it not been for his appearance, she might have yielded to the sudden urge to gnaw on that beautifully manicured nail he'd caressed. Instead she clamped her jaw tight and punched out the number of her New York office.

Geoffrey followed every move, knowing he should leave her in privacy, utterly unable to drag himself from the door. He was intrigued by her sense of self-command as she spoke softly into the phone. Self-command . . . and sitting in his mother's chair, no less.

She fit it well, brought to it a regalness that no one in his family, fine breeding notwithstanding, had possessed. He'd promised to make her a princess; she'd made herself a queen. With that gentle look on her face now as she talked with her second-in-command, he could easily believe that her court adored her.

Who else adored her? Surely there had been men in her life over the years. A beautiful woman, talented, wealthy ... she'd make quite a catch for some man—if, that was, the man didn't mind playing second fiddle to Sara McCray Originals, Inc.

Oh, he knew about her business. A faithful reading of *The Wall Street Journal* had kept him informed of its growth and phenomenal success. He knew that she designed private collections for some of the most exclusive jewelers on Fifth Avenue, that she worked hand in hand with several of New York's most renowned *couturiers* creating jewelry for their semiannual shows, that her one-of-a-kind pieces had been specially ordered and snatched up by one-of-a-kind women from the brightest of political, theatrical and social spotlights.

What he didn't know were the details, and these were what baffled him. How had she done it—sweet, naive Sara, who had never been to the theater before he'd finally taken her in San Francisco? Now she was in New York, most likely attending theater openings as a matter of habit ... if, that was, she spared the time. A pang of sadness shot through him as he wondered whether she'd become the same kind of feminine automaton his mother had been. But no . . . she'd agreed to stay, hadn't she? Cecelia Parker would never have yielded to a personal plea, particularly where the business was concerned.

His jaw taut, eyes grim, he watched Sara nod, smile, offer a final pleasantry to the recipient of her call and hang up. Then he waited guardedly.

Taking a minute to gather her thoughts, she finally looked up to meet his gaze. "I'm all set," she murmured. "David will postpone my appointments and fill in for me wherever he can. Fortunately we're not in the midst of a last minute rush."

"Does that happen often?"

"Not very. I avoid it whenever possible. There's nothing worse than trying to produce a work of art under pressure." She ventured an apologetic smile. "There *are* times when it can't be helped, when a temperamental client decides that something has to be changed or redesigned on a moment's notice. Luckily there's no such emergency now."

An awkward silence ensued, during which both of them assimilated the fact that it was settled, that she'd be staying the night in San Francisco. Then, straightening from the door jamb, Geoffrey approached the desk.

"If you can tell me where you left your bag, I'll have Cyrus pick it up."

"It's over there." Straight-faced, she pointed toward the purse she'd left lying by the leg of the sofa.

"That's all? Your pocketbook?"

"I'd planned on flying back directly," she explained, amused by his dismay. "I've got a few cosmetics in there, and a comb. Otherwise, what you see is what you get."

He idly rubbed his jaw, where the barest hint of a five o'clock shadow only enhanced his masculine flair. "I thought women executives were always prepared for the unexpected."

"I am. I've got a checkbook and credit cards. Anything I need I can pick up. As I recall," she teased, "San Francisco does have stores."

He eyed her for another minute, then shook his head and offered the twist of a smile. "I deserved that. As a matter of fact, you look fine right now."

Despite his compliment, she'd begun to feel a little worn. She'd been in the same suit since she left her apartment in the early hours of the morning. And she suddenly felt tired, as though having decided to stay, she simply couldn't move.

Geoffrey shared that shadowing fatigue.

"Listen," he began soberly, "why don't you go up and take a rest. Help yourself to any of the guest bedrooms. Later we can take a drive along the coast." His eyes clouded. "It might help . . . to unwind . . ."

Sara had no argument. Rising from the desk, she picked up her bag and excused herself. His eyes were on her all the way; she felt them making a clear imprint on her back as she walked through the foyer and slowly made her way up the winding staircase to the second floor.

The passage of eight years hadn't dimmed her knowledge of this house. Turning left, she headed down the hall into the guest wing, then let herself into the last room on the right.

It was her favorite, had always been. Its corner location afforded it windows on two fronts, lending it a brighter, more airy mood. Here she'd felt further removed from the rest of the house, from the repressive tentacles of the Parker life.

To her delight its decor hadn't changed significantly since she'd last stepped over its threshold. Sheer Austrian shades still covered the windows, a bright lemon-hued rug still covered the floor. The same floral pattern of yellows, blues and whites still blanketed the queen-size bed, still sheathed the four walls. The same white-lacquered furniture lent it a provincial air.

It was just the same, still impeccably maintained. She sighed and sank deeply into a cushioned armchair by the window. Head back, she closed her eyes. It seemed so long since she'd done so. She thought of the miles she'd covered this day and knew that the physical distance was but a small part of the journey.

She'd seen Geoffrey again. For years she'd wondered about that eventuality. Their paths had had to cross sometime; if only the circumstances hadn't been this tragedy.

With stark remembrance came an enveloping wave of fatigue. It was only with great effort that she rose from the chair, undressed and sought the relief of the shower. Minutes later, wearing nothing but her bra and panties, she drew back the bedspread and slipped beneath the sheets to fall asleep almost instantly.

Exhaustion took its toll, immersing her so deeply in sleep that she heard neither the soft knock at the door nor the faint click of the latch as it opened. For several moments Geoffrey remained on the threshold. Then, slowly, he stepped inside.

He'd only come to make sure she had everything she needed, but she'd obviously found her way quite well. His footsteps silenced by the plush carpet, he approached the bed, entranced.

She was lovely, lying there on her stomach beneath the sheets, her shoulders bare, their creamy span broken only by the thin-ribboned straps of her bra. Her face was turned away, her hair freed from its twist enough to screen the pillow with its spray of blond silk. He put out a hand to touch it, then drew back with saner thoughts.

Asleep now, without the formality of her business suit or the power of her self-command to remind him of everything she'd become, she was every bit as fresh and innocent as she'd been when he'd fallen in love with her ten years before.

What had happened to their love, to the vows that, despite adversity, it would survive? Yes, she was young . . . but she'd given up too easily. She'd let him down.

With a grimace he thrust a hand through his hair, then left it to massage the taut muscles of his neck. It had been his fault as well. Only recently had he been able to admit that. He'd been young, too, and totally inexperienced when it came to love and its demands. To reason that he'd never *seen* love, that he'd grown up with every luxury save that one, was a pale excuse for the way he'd let her go.

Then, too, having taken for granted his own ability to sidestep his mother's dictates, he'd failed to allow for the full effect the domineering matriarch would have on the uninitiated. Only after Sara had gone had he attacked his mother head on. By then it had been too late to save his marriage.

Self-disgust filled him, to be allayed only by his tender study of the woman on the bed. She was beautiful . . . more beautiful than ever. Even now he felt a familiar tensing in his loins. Had he made a mistake asking her to stay? Could he hold to his word not to push her, when what he wanted most was to shuck his clothes and join her in bed? At least, he mused wryly, her presence had diverted his thoughts.

Not for long. Almost immediately those grave and somber ones flooded back. Alex and Diane were gone . . . his closest friends. And the little one? What was he going to do?

Stiffening beneath the weight of pending decisions, he slowly retraced his steps, looking back only once to see that Sara still slept.

Then, lonely and troubled, he quietly closed the door.

When Sara awoke a full hour later, there was nothing to suggest that she'd had a visitor. Feeling refreshed, she dressed, rewound her hair and repaired her makeup, then headed downstairs in search of Geoffrey.

She found no sign of him in the library or in the front parlor. It was in the larger living room that she spotted him sprawled in a billowing wingback chair before the old marble fireplace.

Clearly distracted, he didn't see her at first but stared broodingly at the cold hearth, with steepled fingers pressed to his lips. She took a step forward, then hesitated, reminding herself of the loss he'd endured, wondering if he mightn't need these moments of privacy. She'd barely turned to leave, though, when he pulled himself from his trance.

"Sara?" He sat forward. "Don't go."

"Maybe you'd rather—"

"No. Stay. Do you feel any better?"

She smiled in response to his gentle show of concern. "Uh-huh, I do feel better. I'm sorry I slept so long. I thought twenty or thirty minutes would do it."

"You needed the sleep." Recalling how

soundly she'd slept while he'd stood by her bedside, he studied the flush on her cheeks. "You look better."

She nodded, feeling oddly self-conscious. He'd looked at her before and she had maintained her poise. Now, though, there was a more personal element in his gaze, an element that reached into the past. She felt young and innocent once more, though the heat in her veins belied naiveté. She was a woman, a mature woman, reacting quite understandably to the presence of an exquisitely handsome man. The chemistry had always been there.

The spell broke when Geoffrey moved. Directing life to his long limbs, he pushed himself from the chair.

"Please don't get up. If you're tired . . ."

"I've got to." He flexed a stiff shoulder muscle. "Otherwise I might take root right here and never move again."

She chuckled softly, remembering him as a man to whom physical inactivity was anathema. "I doubt that." Still, though, there was a note of despair in him that she found downright disconcerting. "How about that drive you promised me? I think we could both use a breath of fresh air."

Fresh air was precisely what they got. With

Geoffrey behind the wheel of his small blue Mercedes, they took the slow, scenic route south along the shore toward Monterey. Neither said much; neither had to. There was simple solace in silence, comfort in quiet companionship. Between the regal sweep of the mountains and the rhythmically pulsing Pacific, their thoughts merged on life, death and the constancy of nature's force.

The sun grew low beyond Sara's window and finally set beyond Geoffrey's shortly after they'd turned and headed back north. When the car's headlights singled out a small roadside restaurant, they stopped for something to eat. It was a token shot at normalcy. Neither was terribly hungry, and what thoughts they shared were quiet and brief.

If Sara had hoped to be able to lighten Geoffrey's spirits, she failed miserably. For the closer they came to home, the heavier his burden seemed, and the silence once more took on the sorrowful air of tragedy.

By the time the car pulled into its slot in the half-empty four-car garage, Sara was as upset as she'd been during the worst moments of the funeral. Her heart ached for Alex and Diane, for Geoffrey, for herself. And she felt thoroughly helpless.

Side by side they walked quietly to the house and passed from the back door through the kitchen into the hall, where they paused to stare mutely at one another. Where did they go from here? There were so many different doors, so many different directions to take. His gaze was troubled; hers was no more clear. Words eluded them both.

Finally, feeling constrained and awkward, Sara wrenched her gaze from his, turned and, gripping the polished mahogany banister for support, climbed the stairs.

Alone in her room at last, she gave up all pretense of poise. Without bothering to light the lamp, she stepped out of her shoes and padded to the window. But the darkness beyond seemed that much deeper, an extension of her inner emptiness, a hollow mirror.

Earlier she'd asked herself what Geoffrey had become. Now she turned the question on herself. In the eyes of the world she was a successful woman, with a business, power, all the finer things in life. Only she knew of those lonely midnight hours when the dreams of yesterday haunted her. Only she knew that those seventy-hour weeks were such by default.

Her eyes sad, she began to undress. She'd

barely hung her jacket in the closet and re-leased the buttons of her blouse when a quiet knock penetrated her distraction. Her head flew up; her gaze riveted on the door. Speech-less, she stared with owl-brown eyes as it slowly, slowly opened.

Three

Geoffrey stood straight and still in the sliver of light that spilled into the darkened room from the hall. Having disposed of his jacket and tie and freed the top buttons of his shirt and its tails, he looked as if he'd been in the process of undressing when a thought had dawned on him. A clean white shirt dangled from his fingers.

Sara stared, unable to move, feeling the light as a tangible thing on the skin beneath her open blouse. Quite against her will she was swept up in a wave of acute sensual awareness.

His eyes never lowered, yet the darkness

couldn't hide their sudden lambency. He'd been her husband once; he'd seen her in every state of undress. But something was different now . . . something . . .

"I thought you could use this"—he cleared his throat to explain—"since you haven't got a nightgown. It's better than . . . nothing."

At the intimacy of his words, Sara felt her insides quiver. Nothing was perfect . . . with the proper counterpoint. Her gaze dropped to the open throat of his shirt, where the hint of his broad chest stole her breath. Then, frightened by the wayward cast of her thoughts, she forced her eyes higher.

His features were taut, made all the more angular by the shadowy light. He looked as torn as she felt—torn between yesterday and today, unable to think clearly about either. But his legs weren't paralyzed, as hers seemed to be. He took one step, then another, moving slowly, irrevocably closer.

Sara's eyes widened as she tipped her face up. Without her shoes she was that much smaller, that much more vulnerable. He stood tall, a breath away, the shirt he'd carried dropped to the bed, forgotten.

Every instinct told her to run—every instinct save two. There was first the need for intoxication, the wish to obliterate momentarily all thought of death and sorrow. And then there was that other need, that more selfish feminine one that craved the feel of this man once more. In eight years she hadn't forgotten the firmness of his flesh, its warmth, the rangy planes of his virility. And his lips, well formed and persuasive—

She shook her head once on the command of saner shreds of thought, but he caught her chin in the crook of his hand and held it gently. When she tried to speak, no words came to protest what she knew was about to happen. In outright disobedience, her pulse quickened to send live currents of desire through her body. This was the inevitable; she was totally helpless to resist it.

His lips hovered over hers for an instant's reacquaintance before touching them lightly. When he opened his mouth wider and sampled her fullness, she knew a blinding surge of heat. Was this indeed the consolation she sought? The events of the day seemed suddenly less raw. Was this the relaxant that the drive down the coast was to have been?

"Sara . . ." he whispered, pausing against her lips for a breath. His hands had risen to frame her face, then slipped gently down to underline her jaw. "Hold me, Sara. I need you just now."

She heard the urgency in his voice, felt the urgency in his body. As she wavered a blunt flash of memory re-created long days of loneliness, longer nights of pain. How hard she'd tried to forget him, delving obsessively into her work . . . but he'd lingered and lingered in her thoughts until she'd tried to salve the ache other ways. It hadn't worked. Her body responded to one man and one man alone.

"Sara?" he rasped.

"I know," she breathed. If he needed her, she needed him no less. The day's sadness may have been the catalyst, but the flame of passion was the substance and the need of eight long years its driving force. Her arms slid up over the strapping span of his shoulders to circle his neck in a binding hold. With her body flush against his, she pressed her cheek to the warmth of his throat and breathed in the male goodness of which she'd been deprived for so long.

Set loose by her melting, he crushed her to him, his arms tightening convulsively, squeezing her until Sara could feel every long, strong sinew of his body. When he drew back, she protested with a small cry, but its sound quickly faded into the depths of his kiss, as did the aching sigh that signaled her final surrender.

If either had felt hesitancy, it was gone now. There was only the overpowering need of two people who shared a past, a sorrow, a fiery mutual attraction.

With the rising tempo of desire Geoffrey deepened the kiss, running his tongue along the inside of her mouth, plunging further for her honey. In wild response Sara opened to him, caring only to obliterate all else in favor of this explosive rapture.

She felt his hands roam her back with growing ardor, felt one arm move higher, one lower. She felt the floor come out from under her when, his mouth pressed to hers, he lifted her and laid her gently on the bed. When he came down half on top of her, she turned into him instinctively.

Were those his hands that moved to her neck, her throat, slid down to steal inside her blouse and cover the fine lace of her bra? Were those her hands that worked feverishly at the few remaining buttons of his shirt and finally spread over the sucked-in flesh of his belly and smoothed their way upward?

In the darkness a mutually insatiable hunger had been unleashed, a hunger ap-

peased only momentarily by the eager exploration of their hands, by ragged gasps and
breathless whimpers. When Geoffrey slipped
her blouse from her shoulders, she did the
same to his shirt. When he lowered his head to
spray fiery kisses down her throat to her
breasts, she thrust her fingers through the
thickness of his hair and held him ever closer.
When he eased down the cup of her bra to take
one rosy areola in his mouth, she felt she might
explode with tension.

"Geoffrey . . ." she moaned, clutching his
shoulders. She closed her eyes and let her
head fall to the side. "Mmmmmmm . . ." It was
half agony, half delight as he toyed with her,
taking her turgid nipple between his teeth and
dabbing his tongue against its very tip. Then
his mouth moved lower and his hand went to
her side to fumble with the button of her skirt.

But patience was a frail commodity. When
the button resisted him, he abandoned it and
whipped himself back up to take her lips in a
consuming kiss while his hips pinioned hers to
the bed. His arousal was complete, his rigidity
electric. She felt charges of excitement surge
deep within her.

Then his breath was hot by her ear, his voice
a thick rasp of meager restraint. "Take off your

things," he whispered, even then rolling to her side to go to work on his belt.

As heated as he, she complied instantly. Her breath came in rapid wisps as she undid the fastenings of her skirt. The echoing rasp of his zipper was enough to send her fever still higher.

One after another, clothes fell from the bed to the floor, bodies twisting and arching to facilitate the task. Sara's eyes never left Geoffrey's dim-lit form; his never left hers. But this was no time for slow appreciation, no time for savoring the rich mellowing of time. The enemy was reality. Neither Sara nor Geoffrey wished to risk its intrusion.

Naked at last, they turned to one another with a melding of the flesh that brought matching moans of pleasure. Her skin felt afire where it touched his; his hands and lips spread the flame further.

The rise of passion was explosive, blotting out everything but imminent bliss. There were soft sighs and ragged moans to complement the rustling of the sheets beneath their writhing forms, but neither spoke a word to break the mindless daze of desire.

Then, with a ferocity that suited them both, Geoffrey rolled Sara to her back and came down between her thighs, finding her, thrusting, reaching the deepest niche of her femininity and burying himself there. She held him with an anguished cry of need, moving only when he did, instinctively adapting to his rhythm. Harder and harder their bodies came together, rising in near-violence to a hallowed peak, then higher once more, higher . . . until the moment exploded in a dazzling, spasmodic display before shimmering slowly down to the reality that neither lover wanted.

It came reluctantly, first with a gradual slowing of the pulse, then with the shifting of Geoffrey's weight to her side. The silence was profound, the dark of night enshrouding. Bit by bit the fact of what had happened tore through the lingering veil of passion.

Sara lay on her back, stiff and unmoving beneath a growing burden of dismay. Only when the pangs of disillusionment grew unbearable did she roll to her side, away from Geoffrey's long male form, and curl into a tight, self-contained ball. She barely knew when he moved to gather his things, only knew moments later that she was alone.

Alone. That was how it had all begun. She'd wanted an escape from the lonely thoughts that had been brought on by the funeral. But that hadn't been all ... and therein lay her mortification. She'd wanted him! Above all, she'd wanted *him!*

Shivering, she drew up the covers, only to find her quakes unrelated to chill. He'd been a drug in her system eight years ago. She'd had to suffer cold-turkey withdrawal then. Whatever had possessed her to yield to him now? she asked herself in bewilderment. Hadn't she learned the lesson once?

Looking back as she'd done hundreds of times, she wondered whether it had been the intense physical attraction to one another that had stood behind their marriage from the start. Oh, yes, he'd been slow during those first days in Colorado when they'd gotten to know one another. But from that night ... from that night ...

How gentle he'd been then; how clearly she remembered it now. He'd led her down a molten path, igniting first one part of her flesh and then another until she'd innocently cried for his possession. He hadn't known she was a virgin. With her whimper of pain he'd stiffened, as though he'd been the one torn apart. His subsequent tenderness had been so thorough that she'd been sure they'd indeed been of one mind, one body. And the glory road he'd taken her on—it had been well worth any bit of pain she'd felt at the start.

Thrashing around now to still the tremors caused by her memories, she tugged the blanket to her chin and burrowed more deeply into the pillow. But Geoffrey's image was not to be escaped as easily. Even tonight in the dark she'd been constantly aware of his identity. To say that any man might have been able to blind her similarly to the day's grief was fool's talk.

Fear. As she lay here alone, it was her one overriding sentiment. She'd finally abandoned herself in Geoffrey's arms; now she must return to New York and forget that this night had ever happened. It had no place in her life, any more than Geoffrey himself did. But having tasted him once more, could she kick the habit again?

The night dragged on with agonizing slowness, the hands of her watch sluggishly crawling from one hour to the next. When she finally slept it was to dream of passion's flight, only to awaken within minutes in a cold sweat of loneliness. The same darkness that had served to help blot out reality when she'd been in Geoffrey's arms now enveloped her in its cocoon of emptiness. Only when the gray light of dawn trickled down onto the windowsills did she dare to slip into a deep, deep sleep.

It was after 'nine when Geoffrey slowly, silently opened the door to find her huddled beneath the covers. Quietly approaching the bed, he lightly tucked back the blanket, then stood in poignant study of her face. It was pale but rested. While he'd paced the floor, she'd slept. But then there were those faint streaks where tears had been . . .

He bowed his head and closed his eyes, absently massaging the aching point by his temple. Then he looked at her again, more sadly this time, before slumping into the chair by the bed to resume his vigil.

She was here. It was hard for him to believe, even after last night. And what had *that* been about? he asked himself, not for the first time. After all that had come between them, why had she given herself to him as she had?

He'd needed her. Sitting now, slouched in the chair, his elbow on its arm, his fist rammed against his mouth, he freely acknowledged that he'd needed her. He could have drunk himself into a stupor. Why hadn't he? Or taken off by himself for a drive into the mountains. Lord knew he'd done that in the past when he'd been upset. But he'd come to her . . . *to her* . . . and, damn it, she'd come through for him. Why? *Why?* By rights, given the way she'd been treated here, she would have been justified had she insisted on returning to New York yesterday. But she'd stayed. Why?

She'd changed. He thought it again. Even in response to his lovemaking, she was a different person than she'd been. Granted, there had been that element of escape for both of them, but there was more. There'd been nothing submissive in her. No, *submissive* was the wrong word. She'd never been submissive, at least not in a negative way. But in the past he'd been the leader, the one to set the pace. Now he half wondered whether, with her darting tongue and her knowing fingers, she hadn't skillfully led them both. She'd managed to drive every thought from his mind but that of her own presence . . . and then she'd turned away.

His eyes glazed in confusion, he continued to stare at her. She'd turned away. It was her right. But *why*, after she'd come this far? What had she thought would happen when she'd wound her arms so tightly around his neck? What had she expected, damn it?

The roughness of his beard grated against the hand he drew across his jaw. He glanced down at the old jeans and sweater he'd thrown on, combed his fingers through his hair and let his head fall against the back of the chair, leaving his eyes heavy-lidded in their lock on Sara's face. His own bore a grave expression, in keeping with his thoughts.

She'd come back. Perhaps it would have been better had she not. For her return had inspired a plan that had kept him awake through the night. Time and again he'd cast it aside; time and again it had wormed its way back into his mind. She'd never go for it . . . or would she? If her business meant all that much to her, she might never agree. On the other hand, if he made the pot sweet enough . . .

Sara stirred then, shifting slightly, sleepily rubbing her cheek against the pillow. She began to stretch, extended one long, bare arm toward the headboard of the bed, opened an eye and froze.

"Geoffrey!" she gasped. Wakefulness was instant. With the realization of her nakedness, she clutched at the blankets as she pushed herself up against the headboard. Her eyes were deep pools of apprehension.

"Relax," he said quietly. "I won't hurt you."

"How long have you been sitting there?"

He shrugged. "A half-hour . . . maybe more."

Staring at him more closely, she wondered where he'd been the rest of the night. With his hair rumpled and his eyes deep and somber, he looked as if he might not have slept at all.

"What do you want?" If it was a repeat performance of last night that he was interested in, she'd have no part of it. If he'd purposely sat himself by her bed looking bleak and in need and . . . damn it, so downright masculine, he'd be in for a grand surprise.

For long moments he said nothing, simply continuing to sit by her side. It was, to his surprise, the most comfortable he'd been since he'd dragged himself from her bed the night before. Her presence, even wary, was a comfort.

At last, with a deeply inhaled breath, he drew himself up straighter. "I want to talk, Sara."

"If it's about last night—"

"What about last night?"

She felt herself falter. "It—it shouldn't have happened."

"Why not? We both needed it."

"I know. But I don't . . . I guess . . . what I'm

trying to say is that it can't happen again. I don't make a practice of doing . . . that."

He smiled slightly. "You mean you don't always tumble into bed with the nearest guy around whenever you're upset?"

"That's partly it." She ignored his mockery to speak with soft conviction. "I also mean that I didn't intend for this to happen when I flew out from New York."

All traces of humor faded from his lips. "I know that, Sara. But I don't think you should agonize over it." He recalled those tear streaks on her cheeks and imagined her remorse. "It happened. That's all. I didn't come here to argue the right or wrong of it with you."

"Then why have you come?" she countered in a whisper. In the wake of his ready dismissal of their passion, she felt inexplicably hurt and truly naked. "What did you want to discuss?"

Geoffrey frowned, feeling suddenly uncomfortable. He'd spent the better part of the early-morning hours searching for the best words. Now they eluded him. Pushing himself from the chair, he stalked to the window, where he stood for several moments with his back to her, trying to decide how best to broach the subject. He'd been catapulted back into the midst of his quandary, and its weight bore down on him.

"Jeff?"

He turned. "I want to show you some—something." He hadn't planned it this way, but maybe it would work. It would certainly be easier than going into long explanations. He took a stride toward the bed and held out his hand. "Will you come with me for a minute?"

"Now? *Right* now?"

"Yes."

She was clutching the blanket too tightly to spare a hand to push the tangle of hair from her cheeks. "But I'm not dressed!"

Geoffrey frowned, then began to rummage beneath the mess of the bedspread that had been so hastily drawn back last night. His fingers emerged, gripping the white shirt he'd brought to her room last night. "Here. This should do it."

She was far from convinced. "I can't wear just—just that."

"We're only going to the other side of the house."

"What—?"

"Please, Sara. Just put on the shirt."

She had no idea what was on his mind; she only knew from past experience that when he had his mind set on something, he was relent-less. And then, when he looked at her that way . . .

"Will you . . . give me a minute?" she asked more calmly.

He nodded, extended the shirt, watched her reach for it. "I'll be waiting in the hall."

With the click of the door behind him, she rose from bed and made for the bathroom, wondering as she freshened up what it was he wanted to show her. Mystified, she put on the shirt, which hung mercifully low on her thighs, saw it safely buttoned, then joined him.

She had no idea how appealing she looked, with her long blond hair flowing smoothly down her back, the fresh white shirt rolled at the sleeves and long, slender expanses of leg extending beneath its tails. She was the pic-ture of simple, unembellished innocence.

Geoffrey felt a hammer thud at his insides. The woman he married, ten years later, look-ing every bit as stunning wearing nothing but his shirt.

"Geoffrey?" She nearly retreated when she caught his expression, but he quickly recalled his purpose.

"Are you warm enough?" he asked, starting at a brisk pace back toward the stairs.

"I'm fine. I feel a little foolish, though. I only hope you know what you're doing."

"I do," he murmured, but he seriously doubted it. Did he really expect her to understand? "We're just going over to the west wing."

"The west wing? Your aunt and uncle were the only ones who used it when I lived here. Where are they now?"

"They've moved south. San Diego."

"Oh."

Having arrived at the central stairway, they turned in stride to the left, bypassing the hallway that branched toward the family's bedrooms—where Jeff's room would be, where their room had been during those years of their marriage—and heading down the hall into the west wing.

As they walked, Sara felt a glimmer of perverse satisfaction. If Cecelia Parker could only see her now! The irony of her dress—or undress—wasn't lost on her. With the finest of designer tidbits in her closets back in New York, Geoffrey's long white shirt was a naughty switch. Eight years ago, though, things had been different. Then Sara wouldn't have dared . . .

"Here," Geoffrey murmured quietly, tipping

his head toward the only open door of four in sight. Without pause he turned into the room. Sara followed more cautiously, and felt justified in her caution as she entered. For if she'd assumed to encounter no one, she had been sadly mistaken.

She found herself in a spacious sitting room, but that was no surprise. She'd known that the west wing consisted of small suites, ideal for aunts and uncles and other relatives who came to visit and stayed forever. The surprise was the woman curled in a chair, reading the morning paper. At Geoffrey's appearance, she quickly moved to stand, only to be halted by his outstretched hand.

"No, no, Caryn. Stay put. We'll just go in for a minute. Is she up?"

The woman was young, perhaps a year or two younger than Sara, dark haired and attractive. She was simply dressed in a sweater and slacks and was either naturally shy or simply startled by Sara's unorthodox attire. She blushed as she answered. "I'm not sure. I just put her in."

Put her in? Sara frowned, forgetting her embarrassment in the face of this mystery. When Geoffrey proceeded to disappear through a half-open door into what she knew to be a bedroom, she turned questioning eyes on the woman he'd called Caryn. The young woman quickly averted her gaze, though, leaving Sara no recourse but to follow Geoffrey.

She approached the door hesitantly, rounded its jamb with her hand on the knob, then stopped still in her tracks at the sight that met her eyes. Geoffrey stood on the far side of the room with his back to her. Her breath caught, then resumed with a gasp when he leaned forward over the high side of a crib.

A crib. A baby. *His* baby? She watched, uncomprehending, as he moved his hand in a gentle circular motion, then straightened and slowly turned. Her heart hammered in alarm when he gestured for her to join him.

She didn't want to. For any number of reasons, spearheaded by a strange foreboding, she didn't want to see what lay in that crib. But she moved, silently, unsteadily, a wide-eyed vision in white with a pallor to match the shirt she wore. When at last she stood beside Geoffrey, she looked once at him before finally daring to look down.

A small child lay on its back in the crib, its thumb in its mouth, its eyes wide and glued to Jeff's. Its pale pink jumpsuit matched its pale pink cheeks to perfection—a little girl from the top of her fine flaxen head of hair to the tips of her tiny bare toes.

Sara helplessly sucked in her breath, only to find breathing even harder when the baby's gaze slid down to meet hers over the button of her nose and her loosely curled fingers. The child's gray-blue eyes never wavered, though her tiny hand quivered with a strong surge of sucking.

Sara couldn't take her eyes from the baby. The face was familiar—so familiar. Was it the universality of infancy? But this child had to be nearly a year old. Her features would bear some resemblance to her parents. Geoffrey— were those Geoffrey's eyes, his cheeks, his chin?

As she stared in half-frantic fascination, the baby rolled to her side and scrambled to her knees, holding her small arms up to Geoffrey, all the while eyeing Sara with trepidation. Ge- offrey lifted her with the ease of a parent and held her comfortably, one arm beneath her padded bottom, the other hand veed beneath her arm. He was neither awkward nor unsure. He obviously knew this child well, and she him.

"Who is she?" Sara asked when she could stand the suspense no longer. The child had happily snuggled against him, her ear to his chest, her thumb gainfully employed in the act of pacification. If only she and Geoffrey had been able to find such simple solace from their grief, Sara mused.

Then her eyes grew wider; her heartbeat tripped. She looked more closely at the child, reached out timidly to touch her soft, golden hair. Familiar . . . so familiar. Dual images superimposed themselves on her mind, producing the tiny face before her. "My God," she whispered, fearful in a wholly different way. "Oh, my God . . ."

Her eyes stricken, she looked at Geoffrey for confirmation. The sadness in his gaze told her everything. Hugging the baby more tightly, he dipped his head to kiss her sweet-smelling forehead, then rocked her gently back and forth. "Sara, this is Elizabeth. Elizabeth Owens."

"Oh, no . . ." Her throat choked with emotion, Sara soundlessly mouthed the words. Alex and Diane had left a child! The tragedy compounded itself. A child—now an orphan. So small, helpless, totally dependent and alone. "Oh, Jeff!" This time she managed a whispered exclamation. "I had no idea!"

"There was no reason for you to have known."

"How old is she?"

"Nearly eleven months."

"And her parents are . . ." She felt her eyes brim with tears and was unable to finish the thought.

Geoffrey nodded soberly. "That's right."

"My God," Sara whispered again as she reached to stroke the child's head. "She's so small . . . so beautiful. I can see Alex in her eyes. Everything else is Diane." She smiled shyly at the child. "Elizabeth. Such a big name for such a little girl."

"They called her Lizzie. They adored her." His voice caught. He buried his head against the child's.

Sara put a soothing hand on his shoulder, only beginning to understand the full extent of his grief. "I'm sorry, Jeff. So sorry. Does she . . . does she have anyone?"

With a long, tired sigh he raised his head and eyed her grimly. "She has me. That's what I've got to talk to you about."

Puzzled, Sara frowned. But the baby chose that moment to turn her face into Geoffrey's chest and let out a soft whimper. "She's tired," he said gently. "She's usually napping by now." He lifted her until the small face was level with his. "Sleep well, sweetheart." He kissed her on the cheek. "I'll be in a little later." Then, with that same practiced ease, he replaced the child in the crib, this time on her stomach, gently rubbing her back for several seconds before taking Sara's arm and guiding her from the room.

Stunned by what she'd seen, Sara couldn't say a word during that return walk to her room. She'd read nothing about a child, but then over the years she'd seen nothing about Alex and Diane save the occasional society picture when they'd invariably been photographed with Geoffrey. She couldn't even recall any reference to a child being made by the minister the day before. But her own distraction had been so great that she might easily have missed something.

Elizabeth. Poor little Elizabeth. The thought of her tragic circumstance sent a chill through Sara, which she tried to ease by climbing back beneath the covers as soon as she reached her room. Geoffrey took up his post by the window, his hands thrust into the back pockets of his jeans. He seemed, if anything, more tense than before.

"I'm sorry, Jeff." Once more she offered soft condolences, at a total loss for further words. There were so many questions she wanted to ask. But she stifled them, hugging her knees to her chest, pressing her mouth to her knees.

"She has me," he'd said. His words echoed in Sara's mind. His genuine love for the child was obvious. Even with the tumultuous emotions of her own discovery, Sara hadn't missed the tenderness in his eyes when he'd lifted the child, the gentle promise that he'd see her later when he'd subsequently put her down.

He'd be a wonderful parent. She saw that now. Had it been true all along, or had the past eight years mellowed him? During the brief stay of their marriage, he'd been constantly on the go. Even beyond the instability of their union, she'd found it hard to imagine him as anything but an absentee parent. Yet yesterday he'd claimed to have wanted children. Had she simply been too young to understand him?

And then, she reflected, closing her eyes and listening to the silence, there was this huge empty house, by rights made for the fun and laughter of a large family. Geoffrey needed that. This, too, she saw. He was alone, and sad. In turn, her heart ached.

She raised her eyes as he slowly turned. The gaze that met hers was fathomless.

"I want to adopt her, Sara."

Her eyes widened. "Adopt her?" she whispered.

"For my own. I want to raise her as a Parker, with every benefit that name can bring."

"But Jeff . . . what about—I mean, there must be some relative who would insist . . ."

His expression hardened. "You saw them at the funeral." She hadn't. She'd been preoccupied with looking for him. "They're older. Their resources are much more limited."

"Resources aren't everything," she reminded him quietly. "My parents had nothing, but—"

"That wasn't what I meant." He cut her off with a wince. "It's partly a matter of a very legitimate stress." When she seemed about to argue, he went quickly on. "Neither Alex nor Diane came from money. Alex was on full scholarship when I met him in college. The money he made through the business was the first of its kind in his family."

That went a long way in explaining the soft spot Alex and Diane had had for Sara. "But—"

"All Lizzie's aunts and uncles are older. Most of her cousins are approaching college age. If that isn't a strain, nothing is. And then suddenly to have the responsibility of a young child again . . ." His voice trailed off meaningfully. "I can handle it. I *want* to handle it."

"But don't they want to? I mean, won't you have a fight on your hands? Can you simply up and claim her? What about a will?"

Geoffrey cast a frustrated gaze toward the ceiling and put his hands on his hips. "A will? Hmmph! Alex never bothered. Maybe it was his feeling of immortality . . . I don't know. A man who's just turned thirty-eight doesn't care to anticipate his wife and himself going in one fell swoop!"

It was Sara's turn to wince, which she did with an added shudder. "It's ironic, when he was a lawyer himself," she murmured sadly.

"A lawyer and my right-hand man in the office. Over the years he'd done well there, not to mention the significant amount of stock he'd acquired. Lizzie is well endowed."

"Which is precisely why one of her relatives may give you a fight," she pointed out as gently as possible. "If there is a trust fund to cover her major needs, doesn't that eliminate the problem of finances?"

The gaze Geoffrey leveled at her was sharp. "*I* know what Alex and Diane would want for their child, not some relative who doesn't even know her. I'm the one who was there the night she was born, who took a shift holding her when she was colicky, who helped rub brandy on her gums when she teethed." He thumbed his chest emphatically. "I'm the one who loves her, damn it! A fight? Oh, yes, I'm sure that once the shock wears off, someone will realize the little thing's worth a bundle. But I'm the only one who wants *her!* And I'm prepared to fight for her!"

Not for a minute did Sara doubt his words. Had the steel gray of his eyes not convinced her, the grim set of his lips or the utter rigidity of his jaw would have. But she wondered if he'd let his emotional involvement get the better of him. He loved the child. Perhaps his fear was simply of losing her.

"Do you think that a relative would try to gain custody of Lizzie purely for the sake of the money?"

"Nah!" He spat the word out and embellished it with a dismissing gesture. "I don't know, Sara. I don't want to think the worst of them and I won't—assuming they don't fight me. They seemed to accept my taking care of her now."

"Has she been here ever since . . ."

"Yes. I brought her here immediately after the accident."

"And yesterday when you disappeared—you went up to see her?" She hadn't been sure why he'd left her so long in the library, had simply assumed him to be occupied with matters relating to the funeral. Now she understood.

"Yes. I wanted to spend some time with her." He lowered his gaze and grimaced at the injustice of it all. "It's heartbreaking, the thought of a child like that suddenly being denied her parents. She may not understand what's happened, but she senses something's up. She's been so quiet, almost as though she knows she has to behave. She *has* to miss Alex and Diane. They never left her other than for a night out every so often." He looked up once more and said with vehemence, "Alex was like a brother to me. Lizzie is family. I want her here."

Sara saw something more as she bore the full force of his gaze: Alex *had* been like a brother to him. Having Lizzie was in its way a substitute for his loss.

But there would be others for whom the loss would be as great. "Didn't either of the families ask about her?"

"Oh, yes. That was one of their first questions."

"What did you tell them?"

"I said that I'd keep Lizzie with me for the time being."

"They didn't argue?"

His short laugh lacked any semblance of humor. "They were relieved. As I said, it's been a long time since any of them had to cope with a squalling infant."

"She's precious!" Sara exclaimed spontaneously. "I can't imagine her squalling."

When Geoffrey's eyes softened, Sara felt a pang of jealousy. "Oh, she has her moments," he said. "Take my word for it."

Sara held his gaze for just a minute before averting her eyes to feign a pensive study of the sheets. He certainly did love the child. There was no mistaking that gentle sparkle. She'd seen it so often herself in those early days of their marriage. But those days were past . . . in spite of what had happened last night.

As a defense against the return of those particular thoughts, she forced herself to think about all that Geoffrey had said. "I don't know," she began softly, looking up more hesitantly. "I can understand and agree with what you want to do." Seeing Lizzie had touched her deeply. Even aside from the fact of her parentage, Sara could understand why Geoffrey would be smitten. "But . . . I just don't know, Jeff. If it comes down to a custody fight, it could be tough. We may have come a long way in the past few years, but it's still got to be difficult for a single male to adopt a child."

The words had no sooner left her lips than an odd shiver shot down her spine. Why did she suddenly feel that the other shoe had yet to fall? Was it something intangible in the air, a sixth sense of her own? Or was it that trace of vigilance about him?

She faltered, unsure, her voice not much more than an anxious whisper. "Why are you telling me all this?" she asked at last. There had to be some reason for his discussing these personal plans with a woman who'd walked out of his life once, indeed, who'd be doing it again today.

"Why, Jeff?"

His eyes never left hers as he approached the foot of the bed. Each step he took heightened the sense of premonition that wreaked havoc with her pulse. When he finally came to a halt he set his shoulders back.

"I want you to marry me, Sara."

Choking on the gasp of a quick-indrawn breath, Sara coughed roughly. Then, her hand splayed across her chest, she eyed him in disbelief. "You're kidding."

He slowly shook his head. "No. I'm dead serious. I want you to marry me."

"Again?"

"Again."

This time it was her head that shook, sending shiny blond strands sliding across her shoulders. But if her equilibrium had been totally overturned, Geoffrey remained the image of self-possession. And that she found extremely disconcerting.

"Why would you ever want a thing like that?" she whispered hoarsely.

"Because I want to adopt Lizzie. And the presence of a wife—a mother for the baby— would make it that much easier."

"Because you want to adopt Lizzie—" Dumbly she repeated his words, her jaw dropping before she clamped it shut. Damn him, she seethed, but he'd been blunt! No pretense, no pussyfooting around. He wanted to marry her for the sake of adopting Lizzie. How totally unromantic; indeed, it was an insult to her feminine pride. What woman in her right mind would accept such a cold-blooded proposal?

"Well, Sara?" His veneer of composure

couldn't hold out much longer in the face of her appalled expression. "Will you marry me?"

"No! And I can't believe you'd even ask it, Jeff! We bombed pretty badly once. It'd be madness to try again."

"I'm not asking for a *regular* marriage. All I want is the appearance of one. How difficult can that be?"

He'd rubbed salt on the wound; she couldn't help but flinch. "It could be *very* difficult, given the fact that I live in New York."

"That could be changed."

Her eyes flashed a molten brown. "Now wait a minute. I've got a life there, and a business! I can't just up and move across the country."

"You managed to come easily enough for the funeral."

"That was supposed to be for one day!" she declared indignantly, then grew suddenly suspicious. "And when did this brilliant idea come to you, anyway? Don't tell me the seduction scene last night was part of it." Feeling half sick to her stomach, she inched back to seek the support of the headboard. When to her chagrin Geoffrey dared to come and sit on the side of the bed, she stiffened her back against its white-lacquered wood.

"No, Sara. It wasn't an act. What happened last night was something very private, just between you and me. There was no ulterior motive involved."

"But it came to you last night, didn't it? I knew there was something in your eyes this morning—"

Sensing a kind of fear in her, he spoke more gently. "After I left you I spent the night thinking. I don't know exactly when the thought came, but it's a good one."

"For *you*, maybe. But not for me. And certainly not for Lizzie."

"Why not?"

"She needs a mother, for God's sake! I have a full-time career, and I know about as much about mothering as—as—"

"As any mother presented with her first child. But that's beside the point. I wouldn't ask you to do a thing, Sara. I'm perfectly willing to be here when Lizzie needs me, and I'll have a nurse—either Caryn or someone else—here to take care of her the rest of the time."

"That's cruel. She needs a mother."

"Damn it, I know that!" he exploded in frustration, sitting straighter, propping himself on balled fists. "But she's just lost her own and I'm trying to find a viable alternative. I want to adopt her, and I want to do it soon. The older she gets, the greater the chance of an upheaval affecting her. Children of three or four can be very astute. I want things settled now!"

Sara bit her lip, feeling not so much shocked as confused. Preposterous as Geoffrey's marriage proposal was, his reasoning had some merit. "Why me?" she moaned. "Why *me?* Surely you can find another woman who'd be willing to—"

"I don't want another woman!" he exclaimed loudly, then lowered his voice to cover the outburst. "What I want," he resumed, choosing each word with care, "is a situation that will facilitate my adoption of Lizzie."

"But *why me?*"

"Because we know one another. Because we've already been through it before and have no delusions about it. Because you're here and you wouldn't have been had it not been for the feelings you had for Alex and Diane." His eyes sharpened in gray penetration. "Is it that much to ask—a token marriage, out of respect for what Alex and Diane would have wanted?"

Four

"That's unfair," Sara whispered, feeling the low blow as if it had been physical.

But Geoffrey refused to back down. "Is it fair that that baby will never see her parents again? And while we're on the subject, let's weigh and balance things for a minute. Let's look at who stands to lose what with your decision." These were the arguments he'd lost a night's sleep to formulate. He paused only long enough for breath before continuing in a deep and determined tone.

"If you refuse, Lizzie may lose the smoothest possible transition from what she had last week to—to whatever she'll have in the future.

In my book that's a pretty big loss for a kid who's lost nearly everything else.

"Now let's take you," he went on systematically. "Obviously you'd rather get on that plane today and return to New York, putting Alex and Diane and everything else about San Francisco in your past. But supposing—just supposing—you agree to marry me: What have you got to lose?"

For a split second she had no answer. Then, reacting to the fear that she might actually begin to consider his proposal, she grasped at the most obvious fact. "My own life, Jeff—it's back there in New York. Everything I am today is tied up there."

"Sara McCray Originals?"

"Yes."

"Open an office here. You mentioned that you'd considered it. Why not do it?"

She couldn't exactly tell him that she'd ruled out the possibility for the very reason of his presence on the West Coast. Should she agree to his proposal, it would be a moot point anyway. "I—it would be too difficult. Everyone's in New York."

"There are a whole lot of people out here, Sara," he chided. "You could increase your business doublefold."

"But I don't want to do that! It's already big enough! That's been the whole point of setting some limits. When too many people own 'originals,' the value inevitably drops."

"Then be selective. You could do it very effectively working from coast to coast." He held his hand up in a gesture of reassurance. "Look, I've thought this all out. In the beginning you could commute to New York every week and return here only for the weekends. That would give us a chance to make our marriage known and to start whatever legal proceedings are necessary to formalize the adoption. In the meantime I could have the guest cottage redecorated."

At its mention, Sara instantly conjured the image of the quaint little house set deep in the estate. Her pulse shot ahead. "The one tucked in the woods?"

"You always liked it," he said more gently.

"I wanted *us* to live there . . . but you kept saying that it was too far from everything."

At her soft accusation, he looked away for the first time. When he stood abruptly it was to pace to the foot of the bed. There, his hands braced on the raised footboard and leaning slightly forward, he watched her toy with a button of the shirt that loosely draped her body as she curled against the headboard. She looked so young, so vulnerable.

"It wasn't my decision to make, Sara. The cottage is part of the estate, and the estate belonged to my mother. As many times as you begged me to move into the cottage, I asked her for its use." His tone hardened. "But she wanted us right here, in the house, under her nose."

Somehow his resentment freed Sara from her need to express any. In its place, though, came perplexity. "Why did I always assume you didn't want to live in the cottage?" she asked, frowning.

"Perhaps because I never explained things as I should have."

"Why didn't you?"

"I was right in the middle, Sara, with you on one side, my mother on the other. At the time it seemed better for me to take the blame for that particular disappointment rather than give you further cause to hate her."

Sara's first impulse was to deny that she'd hated his mother, but for the sake of honesty she caught herself. She *had* come to hate Cecelia Parker, though such a confession was pointless so long after the fact. "I only wish I'd known the truth," she murmured softly, thinking of her marriage, wishing she had better understood Jeff. But it was water over the dam. And now he'd offered to redecorate the cottage.

"It would be a perfect office for you, Sara. You could have several rooms on the ground floor, and the attic could be converted into a workshop."

He really *had* thought it out, she mused with new respect as she pictured a workshop snuggled beneath those gabled eaves. "I don't do much of the actual work anymore," she reflected on the wave of a momentary daydream, "though I'd love to get back to it. It seems that I work mostly with pencil and paper now, creating designs and adapting them to various fashions or personalities."

Her eyes shot back to his when Geoffrey offered encouragement. "You could do whatever you wanted, Sara. Don't you see that? You could set up an office here, have whatever staff you need, visit New York whenever you see fit . . . it could be a nice switch, if you chose to approach it with a positive attitude."

A positive attitude. To her dismay, she could see it on the horizon. "I don't know." She fought its insurgence. "There are still . . . other things . . ."

"Name one."

She looked at him more sharply. If he expected her to yield at the first challenge, as the Sara of old might have done, he was in for a surprise. "My friends, for one." She squared her jaw.

"You'll see them whenever you're in New York, and that could be very often. Name another."

"My . . . social life."

"So there *is* someone?" He'd known there had to be, yet hearing her say so bothered him. He couldn't seem to shake his possessiveness. What a time for it to crop up.

"There are lots of someones," she spoke quietly. "Good friends who know me well enough to be patient and to understand that my work comes first. But there are certain social events that I have to attend."

"I'd take you."

"In New York?"

He gave a facetious smirk. "Unless you could arrange a relocation of the particular event." Then his backhanded humor vanished. "But I would be your husband, Sara. I couldn't allow another man to be your escort— especially in light of the purpose of the marriage. Your being seen with other men would give any court social worker serious doubts as to the stability of the home life we'd be offering Lizzie."

There was a tightness at the corners of his lips that suggested he wouldn't budge on this issue. But then, as she let her mind wander, Sara realized she wouldn't want him to. One part of her liked the idea of introducing Geoffrey to her circle. It was the other part that said she was insane, the other part that forced her to speak up, if only on a diversionary matter.

"But wouldn't a court worker question the setup anyway? I mean, with a mother who jaunts back and forth across country . . ."

He'd given this some thought himself and now spoke more slowly of his conclusions as he ambled back to her bedside. "That's why I'd want you to set up an office here. And that's why, as soon as it's set up, you'd have to spend at least part of every week and weekend here. Many a mother works nowadays. Having the cottage on the grounds of the estate would be ideal. Any social worker would have to be impressed by the ability you'd have to work *and* mother."

Mother. Only as he'd said it that way did the reality of the prospect hit Sara. If she agreed to marry Geoffrey and they proceeded with the adoption, she would actually be a mother. Once more the image of Lizzie's face flashed before her eyes. Lizzie . . . adorable and totally dependent—and hers? It was a frightening thought . . . an exciting one.

Torn by the conflict, she looked helplessly up at him. "I don't know, Jeff. It's still marriage you're suggesting. *Marriage.*"

He lowered his chin. "Why not, Sara? You haven't ever remarried. Were you holding that option open?"

"I have no intention of remarrying!" What with the absurd turn her thoughts had taken in the past day, she should have used the past tense. But she let it go with wishful thinking.

"Then that can't be what's hanging you up." When he slid down to sit facing her, she knew precisely what was hanging her up. It was the thought of being near Geoffrey day in, day out. And on the pretense of a marriage.

"It's the commitment, Jeff. I'm not sure I can go into a marriage purely for the sake of a child. That would be unfair to her."

He clenched a fist against the sheets. "The most important thing is that the adoption go through."

"But what about *us*?" she argued impulsively. As much as she might have wished to be as selfless as he, she couldn't narrow her vision to the child alone. "*We* have futures, too, you know. I'm not all that sure how long I can bear the farce of a marriage of the kind you want." Her words were not only blunt and callous but also deliberately ambiguous. From the hardening of Geoffrey's expression, Sara knew he'd taken them at their most condemning.

For long moments of silence he stared at her, wondering once more whether she had indeed sacrificed compassion for success. Where was her heart, the emotion that had brought her west in the first place? Could she turn from a child this way? Could she turn from *him?*

With a tired sigh he acknowledged that she'd pushed him to the wall. He'd already offered her the freedom to work, had offered to help her actualize her business expansion to the West Coast. There was but one lure left in his reservoir.

"What if we put a time limit on it? Say a year."

"A year?" she asked blankly.

"In the course of a year, barring no unforeseen obstacles, we should be able to get the adoption finalized. Once the papers are duly signed and Lizzie is mine, you can file for divorce. I won't contest it. I'll even throw in—"

"Don't say it!" she exploded, putting her hands to her ears. If she'd thought his original proposition to be cold, this follow-up was positively glacial. "I don't want your money," she said through gritted teeth. "I've got plenty of my own. And I won't—be—bought!"

Geoffrey reached for her hands and forcibly returned them to her lap. "What I was going to say," he went on determinedly, "was that if you choose to seek a divorce at the end of the year but still want to maintain an office out here, you can move from the cottage to a new office building we've got in town."

"It sounds like we're negotiating a contract," she forced in a bitter whisper. He ignored it to complete the thought.

"I'm a businessman myself, Sara. I understand the kind of effort it will take to open an office here in the first place. In light of that, I'll do my best to facilitate whatever move you may want."

She couldn't think that far. She could hardly think beyond the first decision to be made. Worse, she could barely think of anything but the hands that held hers in such a firm yet gentle grasp. He was so close, so appealing. Even his very obvious exhaustion couldn't dampen his blatant virility.

Where did *that* fit into his scheme, she wondered as she breathed in his richly masculine scent. Just how "real" did he want this marriage to be? With a hard swallow she averted her gaze to her hands. But his were right there, more tanned in contrast, bearing those dark wisps of hair she found so enticing. Thoughts of the pleasure they'd found in each other last night came unbidden. Pleasure . . . release . . . escape . . .

He moved his hand to cup her chin and turn her face upward. "It was even better than before, Sara," he courted her softly. "You wouldn't be disappointed on that score."

"But it'd be so phony," she argued against the warm tingling deep in her belly. "Without love . . ."

Clenching his jaw, he released her wrists and straightened. "Like it was last night?" he growled.

"That wasn't—" she began, only to cut herself off. There had been nothing phony about their needs last night and nothing phony in their mutual satisfaction. No, her self-recrimination on that score had to do solely with that taste of ecstasy she'd feared to be a one-time thing. Now, though, if she agreed to marry Jeff . . .

The bed jostled with his rising. "I've had my say," he stated darkly. "You know what I want and my reasons for wanting it. I'll leave you to make your decision."

"Where are you going?" she called in unexpected alarm.

He paused with the door half closed. "I've got to make a fast trip to the office. I'll be back later to take you to the airport . . . if that's what you finally decide." The force of his gaze made a last demand for her compliance before he severed their eye contact with the firm closing of the door.

Sara sat in stunned silence. She stared at the blank expanse of the door. She shifted her gaze to the window. She put the heels of her hands to her eyes, then combed her fingers back through her hair, letting it fall once more to her shoulders with the same inevitability that seemed to shadow this turn of events.

When she'd decided—was it just the night before last—to make the trip west, it had been with a feeling of unfinished business, ghost chasing of sorts. She'd wanted to silently thank Alex and Diane for being her friends. Now it seemed they were asking a final favor in return. Could she refuse them?

Step by step she reviewed the mechanics of

Geoffrey's arguments. To her chagrin, she had to admit that each one had solid footing. Yes, she *could* feasibly make the move to the West Coast; he'd even made it sound simple. Yes, she could keep her New York contacts with frequent trips east. And yes, there was a certain challenge in a properly handled expansion.

But marriage to him? The passage of eight years had brought changes to both of their lives. How could they ever know if they'd be able to get along on a day-to-day basis? They'd been miserable before. Would it be any different the second time around?

But it was different. Elizabeth Owens made it so. She was, after all else had been said and done, the sole purpose for the arrangement. Now Sara paused to consider this fact, wondering if it would be possible to endure a marriage strictly for the sake of the child and her adoption. There was no easy answer to the question—and Geoffrey wanted his answer by the afternoon.

Her knees wobbly at the overwhelming nature of this potentially immediate change in her life, Sara stumbled from bed and sought solace beneath a hot, hot shower. Nothing, though, could relax the tension of her muscles. By the time she was made up and dressed in the same gray wool suit in which she'd arrived the morning before, she wished only to go back to bed. She didn't want to make this decision! Why had it ever been thrust on her?

What if she hadn't returned to San Francisco? she asked her hollow-eyed image in the mirror. He never would have thought of it then, would he? But she had come, partly out of guilt that she'd never told Alex and Diane what they'd meant to her during those months when they'd so obviously been on her side.

Now she faced an even heavier burden of guilt. How could she possibly return to New York knowing that by doing so she'd be lessening Geoffrey's chances for a speedy adoption of Lizzie?

Her hairbrush hit the dresser with a dull thud. Startled by the sound, she looked quickly down. Lizzie. Why did that tiny face keep coming back to haunt her? Could she ever put it behind if she denied Geoffrey's request and returned to her life in New York?

Weighed down by the dilemma, she slowly made her way downstairs. Mrs. Fleming met her before she'd reached the bottom rung.

"May I get you something to eat, Miss Mc-Cray?"

Sara emerged from her trance with a start.

"Excuse me? Uh, no. Well, perhaps some tea ..." She forced a smile. "I'm not really very hungry."

The housekeeper returned an easier smile. "I can't interest you in a fresh croissant?" she coaxed.

"Fresh croissant?" Sara paused. "Come to think of it, that does sound nice." She stepped from the last stair.

"If you'd like to sit down in the breakfast room—"

"Oh, no. I'll eat in the kitchen, Mrs. Fleming." Then, more shyly, "Eating all alone, even in the breakfast room, can be very lonely."

With an obedient nod that whisked away her momentarily enigmatic gaze, the housekeeper proceeded directly to the kitchen, where she presented Sara with hot tea and a warm croissant. Sara was busy looking around the room.

"You know," she remarked, studying the decorative but practical lineup of shiny copper-bottom pans suspended from a frame above the central island at which she sat, "during two years of marriage, I think I could count on one hand the number of times I ate here. Things were run very strictly in those days."

The housekeeper gave a final wipe to the

top of the stove. "I understand that many things were different when Mr. Parker's mother was alive," she replied cautiously.

"You didn't come until after her death?"

"That's right."

"Why was there such a total turnover, Mrs. Fleming? Did Mrs. Parker's staff leave on their own or—"

"Mr. Parker fired them. All but Cyrus." It was a statement of fact, devoid of emotion.

"Do you enjoy working here?"

For the first time in the questioning the woman's face lit up. "Oh, yes. Mr. Parker is as considerate and undemanding an employer as I've ever had. Of course, he's alone most of the time—" She stopped awkwardly, worried that in her spontaneity she'd said something she shouldn't have. Then, realizing that the damage, if any, had already been done, she went on. "Having the little girl here"—her smile warmed—"has brightened things. Mr. Parker plays with her as though—as though nothing's happened." The smile was suddenly gone, but Sara refused to think of the past with the future foremost in her mind.

"He loves her."

"He certainly does. When Mr. and Mrs. Owens"—her breath caught and she spoke more slowly—"used to come over, he'd spend as much time with the baby as he'd spend with them. She squealed and laughed then. I haven't heard her quite that happy since—"

The further mention was one too many for Mrs. Fleming, who quietly withdrew into herself and found something at the far end of the spacious kitchen with which to occupy herself. Sara, too, grew pensive, once more picturing Geoffrey as a father and finding herself pleased with the image. As a husband? That took greater thought, though.

When she had drunk her tea and finished her croissant, she softly thanked the housekeeper and left the kitchen. It was after eleven thirty. She was booked on a flight that was due to depart in little more than two hours. And there was still a decision to be made.

Her feet took her in aimless wandering through the living room, then the parlor, into the library and back to the hall. Did she want to live here again? It was so different now—quiet, infinitely less threatening. For the first time she could see the silent dignity of the place, even begin to appreciate its beauty. Was it the fact of the changing of the guard, or were her eyes simply that much more sophisticated?

Tugging her suit jacket around her, she gave

way to an impulse to walk the grounds. It was a cool day, even overcast, yet the finely kept landscape seemed to sparkle on its own. Here the years had wrought few changes beyond the growth of the trees and shrubs. Again, though, Sara felt a greater understanding for the natural elegance. Was it simply that this was such a total change from her apartment in Manhattan? Or, again, was it a product of her own growth?

As she walked she recalled the times she'd done the same back then. She'd been so very lonely, feeling at times imprisoned within the estate's confines. The friends she'd been offered she had nothing in common with. The friends she'd had before were totally unacceptable. Cecelia Parker had been in so many ways the reigning queen, grudgingly imposing her dictates on the upstart her son had chosen to succeed her as hostess here. At what point had the older woman decided to oust her? In Sara's jaded view it had been from the very start. Any outward show of conciliation must have been purely for Jeff's benefit.

A shudder passed through her body as Sara determinedly slipped from beneath the smothering mantle of the past. When she found herself following the narrow road leading back from the house, she attributed the choice to her highheeled pumps. When, moments later, she found herself on the doorstep of the small cottage that played so heavily in Geoffrey's proposal, she didn't bother with an excuse. Rather, she lent her weight to the front door and, finding it unlocked, walked inside.

It *was* perfect, she mused as she meandered from room to room, trying to remain indifferent, failing miserably. It would be a definite switch from the office in New York where the constant din of city sounds was in keeping with the speed of business there. She paused to listen now, and heard nothing. *Quite* different.

Marriage to Geoffrey? *Re*marriage to Geoffrey? If it sounded absurd, what was even more absurd was that she was seriously considering it! For, aside from this cottage, aside from that baby, there was still herself and Geoffrey. Herself and Geoffrey. Could she bear it, remembering all that might have been once, yet knowing that their liaison would be for only a year? And what after? What would a second parting be like?

One year. One year as Mrs. Geoffrey Parker again. But no, she caught herself with some indignation. This time it would remain Sara Mc-Cray, for professional purposes at the least.

She was her own woman now. Geoffrey seemed ready enough to accept that in exchange for that one year.

Closing the door firmly behind her, she slowly returned to the main house. Then, without pausing to analyze her motives, she headed back up the stairs and wandered into the west wing.

The doors were open, the rooms empty. There was no sign either of Caryn or of the baby. Strangely disappointed, Sara stood for a few minutes by the side of the crib. Aside from the presence of this newly added piece of furniture, the room was no different from any of the other guest rooms. Yes, it was large and immaculate, professionally decorated in broad sweeps of pale blue and apricot, but it was certainly not a child's room. The first thing she'd do if *she* were to be Lizzie's mother—

Catching herself in mid-thought, she rushed from the room, back down the hall and to the stairs. She'd reached the halfway point of the graceful spiral when an odd noise brought her to a halt. Her foot wavered over the next step. She carefully inched it down. Cocking her head and listening, she identified the sound as coming from the direction of the kitchen. As an unknown force bid her head that way, the dull pounding was joined by the more recognizable cry of an angry child.

On the kitchen threshold Sara paused. There, seated in her high chair, so small yet dominating the room, was Lizzie. Her face was scrunched up, her lips drawn down. She fervently clutched a large wooden spoon in her fist. Before Sara's bemused gaze the spoon hovered in the air, hovered in that moment preceding imminent descent—then hovered still as the child caught sight of her.

Mrs. Fleming looked up quickly from her post at the stove. Caryn pivoted sharply from her perch before the high chair. And Lizzie's expression slowly eased from that of unhappiness to a more neutral, sober-eyed stare. Sara had no choice but to step forward.

"That's an awfully loud noise for an awfully little girl," she murmured gently, her eyes held by the child's.

It was Caryn who explained with a crooked grin. "She's just waiting for lunch. Very impatiently."

Strangely enough, though, the child had quieted. She lowered the spoon to the tray and continued to hold it, but there was no more of the frustrated pounding that had first alerted Sara's attention. Rather, she widened her eyes and cast Sara a subtle look of expectation, to which Sara responded by trying to reason away the little girl's heart-rending appeal. It was a conspiracy, she decided, chewing on her bottom lip as she studied the huge eyes, the tiny upturned nose, the sheen of the fine golden hair. A conspiracy. Geoffrey and Elizabeth were definitely in cahoots with one another.

"Here it is." Mrs. Fleming reached for a dish, carefully deposited the contents of two separate pans and a tin-foil bundle and rounded the counter to place the meal and a small cup of milk on the tray of the high chair. Only then did Lizzie look down.

"Mmmmmm," Caryn coaxed her. "Doesn't that look delicious? I'll just cut everything up"—which she proceeded to do—"and you can help yourself." Which Lizzie proceeded to do. Tiny fingers manipulated a piece of hamburger onto the wooden spoon, the wooden spoon was flattened against her mouth, the piece of cooked meat fell to her lap. The wooden spoon fared worse, landing soundly on the floor while Lizzie reached for another piece of meat and made direct contact from hand to mouth.

"Resourceful," Sara said, and grinned,

watching the child reach for a green bean with the same unerring aim. Then, coached softly by Caryn with the housekeeper in pleased supervision, she downed another piece of meat, another green bean, and a third piece of meat before reaching for the buttered roll.

"No more meat?" Caryn asked.

"Or beans?" Mrs. Fleming chimed in a gentle singsong tone. "They're awfully good for you."

But Lizzie had shifted her gaze to Sara once more, with such a knowing look that Sara couldn't restrain a smile. The child was a sharpie, she mused. She knew precisely what was happening. She'd eat that meat, those green beans when and only when she was ready.

Leaning back against the refrigerator, Sara watched with amusement as the meal progressed. For the most part Lizzie fed herself, with Caryn assisting her in drinking from the cup. When a thin white trickle rolled down her chin, Caryn caught it with the bib. When a piece of hamburger flew to the counter, Mrs. Fleming tossed it deftly into the sink. Small fingers placed another bit of meat on the rim of the milk cup; fascinated eyes watched it disappear into the white liquid. A green bean slith-

ered across the floor toward Sara. She stooped
to pick it up and deposited it in the housekeeper's waiting hand.

But the bulk of the meal was soon in the
child's stomach, evoking coos of praise from
both nurse and housekeeper. When a prize banana was offered, Lizzie reached for it eagerly.
Then, to the pained grimaces of both atten-
dants, she proceeded to play with it, squishing
it easily between her fingers, spreading it in
lumps across the high-chair tray, landing small
dabs in her mouth only when she resorted to
sucking an occasional finger.

But she was happy, and that made the mess
worthwhile. Her intermittent child-sounds
were sweet, as was the gentle play of her
hands. And when she raised her face to Sara's
and gifted her with a wide banana smile, Sara
thought she'd melt on the spot. He'd probably
rehearsed this child! It simply wasn't fair!

Forsaking the support of the refrigerator,
she slowly approached the high chair. "I've got
to run," she whispered, bending down to tuck
a blond wisp behind the child's tiny ear.
Soft . . . warm . . . "Bye-bye," she mouthed the
words, then left without looking back.

There was no need. She could see that face
clearly before her. But there was another one

whose image grew in force with each step she took from the kitchen. When all was said and done it would be *him* to whom she'd be married.

Geoffrey. The thought of him brought that familiar stirring, this time on a shimmer of pleasure. It had been so nice last night. Fast and furious . . . but so very, very nice. The supreme act of communion, serving both their needs. She *had* needed him, and not only to blot out the unhappiness of the day. She was a woman. And she felt a strange sense of satisfaction deep inside that overpowered both fatigue and confusion. Perhaps it was time to acknowledge that she'd been alone for too long.

Making her way pensively back to the library, she knew that it was time to make another decision. She walked to the window, put one hand around her middle, the other to her lips, and closed her eyes. New York: busy, exciting, rewarding—but lonely. San Francisco: busy, exciting, rewarding and—and . . . ?

She didn't know how long she stood there see-sawing between the options. If one side was more heavily weighted with pluses, surely she'd lean that way. But the momentum of the seesaw kept her moving, sliding helplessly back and forth.

Opening her eyes, she stared bleakly at the gray-green of the landscape. Things had happened so suddenly. But wasn't that the way of life . . . and death? In the instant she was besieged by the same pall of fear that had settled in at the funeral the day before. Alex and Diane had died in their prime, having just begun to taste the honey of existence. Life was too short, often tragically short when there were so very many things to do, to experience, to share.

She eyed her watch, then looked back outside. She cast a glance once over her shoulder, turned and went to the phone. She lifted the receiver, hesitated, replaced it. Her gaze focused on the ceiling, then lowered.

Life *was* too short, too filled with dreams that were destined to remain unfulfilled. But was destiny in a rare instance flexible? Was she being given a second chance?

With Geoffrey's face foremost in her mind, she raised the receiver again, this time pressing it to her thudding heart for a final decisive moment. A second chance. Was it? Could she afford to turn it down?

The decision was made on a sudden wave of clarity. In essence, she'd been offered a year with Jeff, a year on new footing, a year in which to try to capture all that she'd wanted once and lost. Never over the years had she forgotten those glorious dreams she'd had in his arms in Colorado. Granted, the facts were different now. He had independence, she a career. They were older, wiser. And though there was no mention of love now as there'd been then, she owed it to herself to give those dreams a final shot.

Impulsive? Yes. And for the second time, no less. But last time she'd been young and dependent, with everything to lose. Now she had her business. She *was* her business. Should the year with Jeff be a dismal failure, she'd still have Sara McCray Originals and the life she'd built for herself in New York.

Perhaps Geoffrey was right. She'd approach it all with a positive attitude. The year would be a challenge, an adventure. It wasn't every successful career woman who had a husband and child served up on a silver platter. As for love, she had no delusion as to its existence. And without delusion, she couldn't be hurt.

Or so her reasoning went as she calmly called the airport and booked a seat on the flight returning from New York early Saturday morning. When she replaced the receiver with the commitment made at last, she turned to find Geoffrey standing at the door.

Even though he was freshly shaven and looked dashing in a dark business suit, with a trench coat thrown over his arm, he was obviously exhausted. But his stance was erect and strong. "You've made your decision?" he asked, his voice a taut rumble.

She had, and she felt suddenly stronger. Squaring her shoulders in her most executive pose, she looked at him. "Yes. I'll have to go back to New York today to break the news and start making arrangements. But I've made reservations to return here on Saturday." She took a deep, deep breath, an expression of relief at having reached such a profound decision. "Your offer is too good to pass up, Geoffrey. Yes, I'll marry you."

She'd never know just what he'd expected, for his face was a mask of impenetrable control. "Are you sure?" he asked evenly.

"Yes."

"And you'll stay with it for a year?"

"Yes."

Impassively he glanced down at his watch. "I'd like to go up to see Lizzie for a minute. Then I'll drive you to the airport."

"If you're tired, Cyrus can—"

"I'll be right back." And he was gone.

Within ten minutes they were on their way. What conversation there was might have been part of a business conference. "If you can bring back an outline of what you want done, I'll have a crew start work on the cottage on Monday. Also list what materials you need."

She cast him a sidelong glance. "I know the suppliers. It would be easier if I ordered directly."

He didn't once take his eyes from the road. "Then be sure to bill me for everything you buy."

"I will not!" she replied in a burst of indignance. "This is a branch of *my* business. *My* company will foot the bill."

"That's not the deal."

"It is now."

He sighed and flexed his neck. "Great start," he murmured, so softly that Sara might not have heard had the traffic been heavier. She felt the need to make him understand her feelings. There was so much they hadn't said before.

"Listen, Jeff," she began, turning slightly in her seat to face him. "Sara McCray Originals is my baby. I created her, I nourished her and I'm as proud of her as any parent could be." She saw the slight narrowing of his eyes but chose to attribute it to a sudden thinning of the cloud cover. "And part of that pride is the knowledge that the business is . . . independent."

"You mean that Parker Enterprises has no finger in it?"

"I mean that *no* other company has a finger in it. I want it to stay that way."

The finality of her words carried them through a period of silence. When Geoffrey spoke again, though, he was no less firm. "The cottage belongs to me, Sara. I'm going to insist on doing whatever structural work is done. You can equip it if you like, but you're going to have to give on the larger work."

Her lips twitched. "If it's your cottage, I guess I'll have to pay rent for its use."

"Hell, no! You'll be my wife! Don't forget that."

"There are many husbands and wives who are on each other's payrolls. What difference is there if I pay you rent?"

With a quick glance over his right shoulder, Geoffrey veered toward the breakdown lane and came to a full stop. Then he turned to Sara and scowled. "The difference is my pride,

Sara. And I can match you ounce per ounce. You may consider this marriage a farce, a business deal. But I consider it something more." Obviously so, if his present intensity was any indication. "While I'm your husband, I'll take care of you." He held up a hand when she opened her mouth. "Fine. You handle the everyday workings of your business. I'm busy enough with my own not to be able to interfere. But let's get something straight. When it comes to clothing and food and everyday expenses, I foot the bill."

"But—"

"No buts about it!" His eyes were steel-hard. "I may have been too young last time to stand up and fight for what I thought was right, but I've come a long way since then. I'll respect your pride; you respect mine. Understood?"

In the face of his vehemence, she sensed that if she shook her head the entire deal would be off. And with a surprising vehemence of her own, she knew she didn't want that. In effect, he was being very reasonable. Swallowing hard, she nodded.

"Good."

That was all he said until they reached the airport. Ignoring Sara's suggestion that he simply drop her at the terminal, he insisted on parking and waiting with her until it was time for her to board.

"I'll . . . I'll see you Saturday then?" she asked, turning unsurely to him. Despite the distance that seemed to have wedged itself between them, there was still last night . . .

"I'll be here."

She nodded and turned to go, but he caught her arm and held her back. When she looked questioningly up at him, she saw that his gaze had softened. And for the first time since she'd agreed to be his wife, it all seemed real.

"Sunday?" he began, then cleared his throat. "Shall I plan the wedding for Sunday?"

She felt her insides quiver at that tiny spark in his eye, felt her throat tighten with emotion. In a silent avowal of her commitment, she nodded. Then, feeling her arm free once more, she turned and headed for New York.

Five

*H*e watched her until she disappeared from view. Then he positioned himself at a huge window and waited as the plane was readied for departure. She was leaving—but she'd be back. Half in disbelief, he slowly shook his head.

He had to hand it to her. She'd come through for him . . . again. First yesterday, then last night, now today. After the way she'd fled in defeat eight years ago, her acceptance of his proposal was the last thing he would have imagined once he'd accepted the fact of her return. It had been a long shot—but he'd been desperate.

His eyes more pensive, he gazed back toward the boarding gate where they'd parted minutes before. She had looked so very sure of herself that again he had trouble conjuring the image of the total innocent she'd been when he'd first met her in Snowmass. Self-assured, sophisticated—she was that now and more. He could only begin to imagine her as the chairman of the board, the president of her own company.

An unbidden surge of pride was quickly supplanted by doubt. She'd changed so drastically since he'd known her last. Would they be able to make it through the year? According to his plan, there would be weekends when they'd be in each other's company constantly. Would it be pure torment, rationalized solely for the child's sake, or might it be pleasant, as yesterday in its sad way had been, even evolve into something?

He followed the progress of the plane when it glided slowly backward, edging away from the terminal. What was "something"? What did he want it to be? Damn it, he just didn't know! He only knew that he'd been torn by conflict since he'd first seen her yesterday. Admiration and anger, attraction and resentment, respect and disdain . . . the war continued.

Her business meant everything to her. That much was obvious. His lips thinned at the irony of it—Sara becoming the kind of person his mother might have wanted as a daughter-in-law. Once again he wondered if Sara would be as heartless, as self-centered. She'd been so warm once, so adoring.

His brooding gaze tracked the plane as it rolled heavily onto the runway. What was it she'd said, he asked himself, administering a hand to the crick at the back of his neck. She'd called his offer too good to pass up. It must have been the time limit that had finally won her over. In that time she might easily establish her business on the West Coast so that a simple relocation from the cottage to the city—to any western city—would be a snap. Granted she'd refused the bulk of his financial aid, but between the cottage and her connections as his wife, she'd do well.

His eyes narrowing, he watched the plane disappear in preparation for its final thrust. A negotiated marriage—the last thing in the world he wanted! There were times when he hoped never to see another conference room, never to negotiate another deal, never to sign another contract. Now he'd all but offered to have his lawyer draw up a prenuptial agreement. Thank heavens she hadn't pushed him to that.

Damn it, but Sara had this way of tying him up in knots. After having thought never to see her again, to find her here with him . . . and she'd felt so good in his arms last night. But then that had always been the case. Flesh against flesh they'd never failed one another. It had been only when they'd dressed again, he in his signature sweaters, she in her basement bargains, that their worlds had clashed.

He inhaled deeply, drawing himself from the past with the realization that this time they were approaching marriage on an equal footing. No longer could he picture her young and impressionable, the pauper of the pair. No longer could he assume she'd yield to his every wish. Hadn't she proved that no more than thirty minutes ago with her insistence on the independence of her business?

Sara McCray Originals. Her baby, as she put it. Perhaps that business *was* all she needed in life. But, damn it, he cursed as he slammed a palm against the railing, she'd promised him a year of that life, and a year was what he'd get! At its end she'd have her West Coast connection and her freedom. He would have Lizzie. Wasn't that all he wanted?

His eyes dark and faraway, he allowed himself a moment's recollection of the dreams he'd had once. In Sara he thought he'd found the antidote to his sterile existence, a woman who embodied the heart and soul his barren life had lacked. He moaned softly. He'd loved her so—it still hurt. But it was over.

Over. Beginning again. The key, he firmly told himself, was to expect nothing. He'd take her for what she was and refuse to let her get to him. Very sane. Very cool. Very simple.

Standing that much straighter before the window, he caught sight of the plane as it sped down the runway and lifted nose first off the ground. His jaw set, he followed the plane until it was no more than a distant silver speck. Then, drawing energy from a basic reserve, he turned to see to all that would need to be done before another plane returned her to him on Saturday.

He was standing in nearly the same spot when the plane touched down. At the loudspeaker announcement he headed for the designated gate, where he stood and waited, patiently at first, then with mounting worry as the passengers filtered through without sign of Sara. She wouldn't have changed her mind, certainly not without having called him, he assured himself. Then, too, she'd have called if she'd been delayed and had missed the flight.

With growing unease he shifted his stance. Everything had been arranged; they were to be married in the morning. Perhaps he should have called her last night after all, just to verify things. He'd looked at the phone any number of times until reason had finally won out. If it was a business deal they'd agreed to, he'd behave with his usual confidence. Of course she'd be here. Sara McCray Originals hadn't earned the respect it had with its founder and president missing engagements. And it was a crowded flight; there were still many passengers to deplane.

It seemed an eternity that he stood watching, waiting, wondering how she'd look, what she'd wear, then berating himself accordingly. By the time she finally appeared, he was, to his chagrin, far less confident than that usual business self of his. He took in the neat twist of her blond hair, her silk blouse and tailored wool pantsuit, her fine leather purse and much larger shoulder bag, the alpaca coat over her arm. And then she looked up and he sucked in a ragged breath. She was positively elegant, walking with such natural grace and every bit of the self-possession he seemed at that moment to lack. In another situation he'd have liked nothing better than to be a fly on the wall, watching her longer, admiring that air of serenity she'd brought with her from New York. But she was looking for him. And he didn't want to keep her waiting. Straightening, he moved forward to catch her attention.

She saw him instantly. Her eyes met his; her step faltered, then continued. By the time she'd reached him she wore the gentlest of smiles. "Hi, Jeff," she breathed, so softly that he wondered whether seduction was a normal business ploy of hers. The thought was a timely reminder of the purpose of their reunion.

"How are you, Sara?" He transferred the bag from her shoulder to his own, then looked down at her. *Damn*, but she did look lovely.

"Fine," she answered.

Taking her elbow, he guided her from the crowd. "Good flight?"

"Uh-huh." Her smile persisted. He noticed that her lips were freshly glossed, her cheeks just pink enough, her eyes neatly lined with a smudge of charcoal.

"You must have had to get up at dawn. Are you tired?"

She shook her head. "I managed to sleep

some on the plane. I guess I'd better get used to doing that."

A swift pang of guilt shot through him. What he'd asked her to do—to commute between coasts—was apt to be a strain on her. He'd just have to make sure she got enough rest on the weekends.

"Uh . . . you do have another bag this time, don't you?"

Her laugh was little more than an apologetic tinkle. "I'll say. It's pretty big; they insisted I check it. I usually try for just carry-ons, but . . . well, I thought I ought to leave as many things as possible here."

"No problem," he assured her placidly. There was no rush. No rush at all. They had a full year, beginning tomorrow.

The wedding was nearly as simple an affair as the one that had taken place ten years before. The bride and groom were the same, as was the wide gold band that Geoffrey placed on Sara's finger. There, though, the similarities ended.

The brief ceremony took place in the library. It was poetic justice, Sara had mused when Geoffrey led her there. Could Cecelia Parker see them now, or was that shaking of the floor nothing more than the trembling of her own knees?

Geoffrey stood by her side, looking positively handsome, dressed in a navy suit that emphasized the breadth of his shoulders and the tapering of his body to a lean width of hip. His shirt was white and crisp, his tie a bold crimson-and-gray stripe. In Sara's biased view he seemed taller, more stately than ever. And she felt a kind of visceral anticipation at the thought of his being her husband again.

The judge who married them was a friend of Geoffrey's, a man whose vague familiarity with the facts of the situation dictated his gravity. Standing in witness to the event were the chauffeur and the housekeeper. And in one corner of the large leather sofa, being carefully watched by her nurse, was Lizzie, whose child-size realm of attention went little further than the fluffy stuffed kitten Sara had brought her from New York. More so than anything else, the child's presence was silent testimony to the uniqueness of the circumstances.

In her hand Sara carried the single white rose Geoffrey had given her when she'd reached the bottom of that long winding staircase. She held it gingerly, mindful of its thorns, its symbolism far from lost on her.

She wore a blue silk dress that she'd bought the day before and looked stunning by any standards. Its deep V neck, long sleeves and sashed-in waist molded her gentle curves to perfection. At her ears were gold drop earrings embedded with sapphires, at her throat a matching choker. They were Sara McCray Originals, as was the ring she'd given to Geoffrey.

Until the moment she finally slipped it on his finger, she hadn't quite believed he'd wear it. He'd never worn a wedding band the first time around; he'd never worn rings, period. She had sketched the design on the flight back from San Francisco, had set her finest goldsmith to work on it the very next morning. And she'd been pleased with the outcome: a very masculine band of gold into which was hammered a pattern of subtly intertwining ridges. Only when she'd broached the subject to Geoffrey had she had doubts.

It had been the afternoon before. They'd gone straight from the airport to the house to spend time with the baby, then at Geoffrey's firm suggestion had headed into town to shop. Over her vocal protest, he'd insisted on buying her half a wardrobe to complement that other half in New York and eliminate the need of her carrying much of anything back and forth on the plane. Only when the trunk of the Mercedes was filled had he allowed her to stop, taking her for a light snack in Ghirardelli Square.

It was the first free time they'd had to sit and talk. Geoffrey had taken the opportunity to outline the plans he'd made for the wedding. When he brought up the issue of the wedding band that he'd had in his possession since she'd removed it from her finger eight years before, she took advantage of the opening.

"Jeff . . . I . . . I'd like to give you a ring."

He looked at her uncomprehendingly. "A ring?"

"A wedding band." She held her breath, pending his response. But if he'd been taken by surprise, he quickly regained control.

"That's a—novel idea." His half-grimace said little.

"Many men wear them. And I just thought you might . . . I mean . . ." Whatever the reasons, she wanted him to have something she'd created, but she couldn't say it quite that bluntly. "What I'm trying to say," she resumed with a sigh, "is that if this is a marriage for show, we might as well do it right. All the trimmings, so to speak."

He stared hard at her. "What's right for the goose, is that it?"

"Of course not!" she exclaimed, then caught herself and met his gaze head-on. If he could be hard, so could she. "But now that you mention it, you've got a point. If you expect me to wear a wedding band, surely you won't object to wearing one yourself."

"You never asked me to wear one the first time."

"It didn't occur to me then. Things are different now." Quite. She paused. "Well?" she asked more quietly, trying to hide how much it mattered to her.

His voice, too, had gentled. "Is it one of yours?"

"Yes." She lowered her eyes to fidget with a spoon. "I designed it for you after I—after we reached our . . . agreement."

"Then I guess I have no choice, do I? I can't very well turn down an original."

Had there been mockery in his voice, she might have happily spilled her vanilla frappe over his dark gray gabardine slacks. But there was nothing unkind in his tone, though she couldn't tell whether he was actually pleased or simply being conciliatory. Either way, she was satisfied.

Now, as she looked down at their intertwined hands, she was even more so. The ring was perfect for him, heavy enough to exalt his masculinity, light enough to bear a strange thread of optimism. Rather than being a symbol of servitude, it was a tribute to their union.

"You may kiss the bride, Geoffrey."

The judge's words took them both by surprise. Both pairs of eyes darted from their hands to a higher meeting point. Then Geoffrey lowered his head and kissed Sara with such slow gentleness that she felt every bit the new bride. It was ridiculous, she told herself, but there was a sense of excitement, an unexpected lump in her throat . . .

Then there was champagne and caviar to go around, and an equally unexpected toast offered by the judge. Looking from bride to groom, he raised his glass. "To the fulfillment of your dreams—separately, together."

Not daring to look at Geoffrey for fear her own dreams were etched in her gaze, Sara softly thanked the judge and sipped her champagne. It was only later, after Lizzie had been fed, played with and put in for her nap, when she and Geoffrey were alone at last in the large dining room awaiting a wedding luncheon, that she commented.

"Judge Symmes was very . . . thoughtful."

"He's been a friend for years."

"How much did you tell him?"

"He knows that we were married before and that we want to adopt Lizzie, but that's about all."

"Did he know Alex?"

Geoffrey nodded more sadly. "He knew them both."

Mrs. Fleming appeared with a tureen filled with a delicately spiced acorn squash soup, which she proceeded to ladle into waiting soup bowls. Sara watched distractedly, thinking once more of Alex and Diane, hoping she'd made the right decision regarding their child. When the housekeeper had vanished once more, she spoke her thoughts.

"What does he think of the adoption?"

"He approves."

"Does he think we'll have any trouble?"

Geoffrey looked up from his soup. "Why should we? For all outward purposes we're the ideal couple. We've got our youth, our fortunes and plenty of love for that child."

"But the marriage—won't its suddenness tip somebody off?"

He denied the probability with a facetious shrug. "The story is heart-rending, when you stop to consider it. We were married once when we were very young, we split up to give each other time to grow, and now, brought together by our mutual grief, we've decided that we need each other desperately." He paused for a second to cast her a keen eye. "No one will know any differently."

"Except us, of course," she prompted. It seemed important to remind herself that this *wasn't* a storybook romance.

"Of course," he echoed wryly, then turned his attention to his soup. He looked up again only when Sara called his name.

"Jeff? What about the adoption?" She knew so little about the procedure and what would be expected of her. When she'd agreed to marry Jeff her mind had been on other things. "What does it entail? What will we have to do?"

He studied the gently waving pattern of his soup as he moved his spoon through it. "Technically Lizzie is a ward of the state right now. I've already had a lawyer file papers for temporary guardianship. What we have to do next is apply for the actual adoption."

"It's all done through the courts?"

Glancing up, he caught her note of apprehension and seasoned his voice with a corresponding dash of reassurance. "Yes. There will

be a slew of forms that we'll have to fill out.
And there'll be interviews with social workers.
The attorney I've hired is a specialist in family
law. He'll try to expedite things as much as
possible, but there's only so much he can do.
The courts won't rush into this kind of thing."
His lips formed a twist of sarcasm. "It's that
nine-months-to-grow-it philosophy."

"I see," she said, averting her eyes. She
wondered if he wasn't thinking again that she
hadn't wanted children, then wondered
whether she wasn't just feeling guilty. Guilty?
Was it her fault that something had gone awry
in her body? But that was inconsequential
now. It looked as though, for the year at least,
she'd actually have a child. Legally, once the
adoption went through, she *would* be Lizzie's
mother.

Geoffrey's deep voice broke into her reverie.
"Thanks for the gift you brought her, Sara. It
was sweet of you."

"It was nothing."

"That's not true. You didn't have to get her
anything. I know how busy you are."

"Really, Jeff, it was nothing."

But he seemed to be gaining momentum en
route to making a point. His eyes grew more
intense; his brows lowered to narrow their

beam. "This is a marriage on paper. I want you to know that I don't expect anything of you other than your physical presence here and there, and your cooperation when it comes to the forms and interviews."

Sara felt clearly wounded. "Such romantic talk . . . and on our wedding day, no less."

Her defensive humor didn't amuse him. The squash soup was forgotten. "I mean it, Sara. I'm trying to be fair. You've got your life and it's a demanding one. Just as long as I get Lizzie—"

His words died in the face of her appalled expression. "What kind of hard-hearted person do you take me for?" she cried, leaning further away from him. "Can't you give me credit for feeling *something* when I look at that child? I'm not inhuman, you know. Don't you think I enjoyed buying her that kitten?"

"I don't know. Did you? I suppose F.A.O. Schwarz *is* on the way to Cartier's."

Unable to believe his callousness, Sara gasped. Unable to find a suitably acid retort, she bit her lip. Unable to still the fine tremor in her limbs, she held to the arms of her chair for steadiness, all the while wondering if this was an omen of things to come. Feeling suddenly chilled, she transferred her grip to her middle.

Then, quickly gathering her thoughts, she spoke quietly, slowly, in amazing control.

"There's something you obviously don't understand, Geoffrey. In two years of marriage to you I had it to here"—she made a slice at the tip of her nose—"with doing things that were expected of me. When I left you I vowed to live life the way *I* wanted. And that's the way it's been since. If you interpret that as selfishness, that's your choice. But I don't see it that way." Breathing hard under the strain of control, she paused for breath. Her own eyes narrowed in anger. "The way *I* see it is that I'm a free woman—free to do and feel according to my own conscience. When I agreed to marry you it was my free choice to make. Same thing when I agreed to be a mother to Lizzie. If I want to buy something for her, I will. If I want to take her out for a walk, *I will*. And while we're on the subject, I have every intention of redecorating that room! Lizzie needs a child's room, with bright colors and pictures and mobiles and toys to stimulate her."

"I'll see to that."

Her eyes widened in rebuke. "*I* will!"

"When?" he growled. "You'll be in New York most of the time."

"*You* were the one who talked of how simple

it would be, with jet planes and telephones and all," she mocked, but more gently now as her anger mixed with perplexity. Geoffrey expected the worst of her. Why? "I can do it. I *want* to do it." She paused, then asked softly, "Isn't it a mother's prerogative?"

Her words hung in the air. Geoffrey stared at her in confusion. Confusion? In turn, Sara couldn't understand that. Finally, deadlocked, they averted their eyes and quietly finished the soup. Responding on cue, Mrs. Fleming cleared the dishes, only to return moments later with salads for them both.

Sara stared at the carefully arranged assortment of greens for a minute, reached for the smaller, outer fork of two to the left of plate, then chuckled. "This brings back memories." She looked up and around the elegant room. "For years the mere thought of this room was enough to kill my appetite. I'll never forget my first meal here." She shook her head. "Pure terror. There was so much I didn't know."

"It wasn't your fault," came the deep reply.

"No, but that was small solace for my humiliation. I had no way of knowing that this," she raised the small fork, "was for salad while the other was for the main course. We didn't learn these things back home."

"You covered up very well."

She shot him a punishing glance. "*After* that first debacle. By then the damage was done."

"It wasn't that bad."

"Not to you. *You* weren't the one whose ego was being torn to shreds."

"No," he mused pensively, then lapsed into silence. He, too, remembered that first meal. He'd known of her tension and had done whatever he could to ease it. Why had it mattered which fork she'd used? She'd been polite and well-spoken, had done her best to conform to what the others were doing. But his mother had made it a point to embarrass her. Oh, he remembered it well. Even the fact that the older woman was gone now did nothing to mitigate his anger.

"Well," Sara began on a more positive note, "you can rest assured I know what to do this time. I've studied all the proper books, apprenticed with all the proper people. This time around your mother would have been proud—"

"That's enough!" Geoffrey exploded, causing her to jump at the unexpected strength of his response. But he quickly controlled his reaction, knowing it to be misdirected. "I *never* questioned your ability on that score, and I have no intention of doing so now." He cleared his throat and sighed to signal the end of that particular discussion. "What I *would* like to know is what happened in New York."

It took Sara a minute to shift gears. "In New York?"

"You did break the news to your people there, didn't you?" When she nodded, he went quickly on. "How did they take it?"

She took a bite of romaine lettuce, chewing it as she recalled that first bombshell of a meeting at which she'd faced her fellow executive officers. She'd called an impromptu meeting of the board for the following day. The reactions were the same. "They were . . . shocked."

"Was that good or bad?"

"Let's just say that it was awkward for a while there." Awkward; she was becoming a pro at handling awkward. Lately it had seemed her shadow.

"Why?" he asked, genuinely interested.

She noted the way his lips had relaxed at last, recalled how gently they'd kissed her, tore herself from that thought to the present with a silent scold. "It's a change—a big one. They were bound to feel threatened."

"Exactly what did you tell them?"

"I told them that I was going to open a

branch in San Francisco, and that I'd be commuting back and forth."

He arched a brow. "You didn't say you'd be married?"

Feeling distinctly cowardly, she frowned and studied the bright shine of her fingernails. "I . . . I thought I'd wait until tomorrow."

"Why, Sara? Why didn't you tell them at the start?"

Mrs. Fleming's appearance couldn't have been better timed from Sara's point of view. It gave her an added minute to come up with an excuse. Unfortunately she needed more than the time it took to replace the remains of salad with matching platters of filet mignon, fresh broccoli with hollandaise sauce and wild rice. When she and Geoffrey were alone once more, she was as much at a loss as she'd been before.

"This is beautiful," she began with a speculative eye on the new presentation. "Mrs. Fleming is a wonder—"

But Geoffrey would have no part of her diversionary tactic. "Why didn't you tell them, Sara?"

She took a deep breath and exhaled it slowly. "To be very honest, I wasn't up to going into detail. There was enough of an immediate nature that had to be done. And they had scores of questions even *without* my mentioning our marriage."

His mind had begun to sort things out. "They don't know that you were married once."

"No."

"And you didn't want to tell them?"

"It's irrelevant. These are my business associates. Much as I value their friendships as well, I try to keep my private life private."

"But you *will* tell them..." He seemed strangely unsure, in turn evoking Sara's reassurance.

"Yes. I will tell them." She straightened her left hand and studied the wide gold band on that finger that had been bare for so long. "They'd be bound to notice, anyway. I never wear rings."

He eyed her dubiously. "You're kidding." Her simple head shake failed to settle the matter. "You mean that you make them all the time but never wear them yourself?"

"Earrings, necklaces, bracelets—yes. Rings—no."

"Does it bother you to wear that one?" He shot a glance at the gold band in question.

Sara followed his gaze. It was precisely because of that one, its memory and significance, that she'd never worn another ring. She wiggled the finger as if testing its weight. "It may take a little getting used to, but no, it doesn't bother me. Wedding bands are . . . different."

Her voice was soft, her eyes wider when Geoffrey looked back at her. For an instant he seemed mesmerized by something, then he shifted his sights to his own hand. "Thank you, Sara. I like the ring very much."

When he looked up, she caught her breath. He was her husband—devastatingly handsome—and the attraction between them was as strong as ever. A simple look from him and she relived the passion they'd shared. Her pulse raced, and her cheeks flushed. And she wondered what would happen this night. It was the only thing they hadn't settled.

But Geoffrey was reluctant to remedy that now. With a deep breath he sat back. "Tell me about the plans you've made for the office here," he ordered quietly.

She didn't fight him. When it came to Sara McCray Originals, she was on the safest ground possible. As they ate she told him of the meetings she'd held in New York, the input she'd received from her staff, the preliminary plans she'd made. He, in turn and to her pleasure, offered several valuable suggestions regarding the best way to approach the San Francisco community.

For the first time that day they both relaxed. For Sara it was a welcome change from the previous days of soul searching, of doubts and second thoughts. Sitting there talking in perfect harmony with her husband, she could almost believe it was for real. And to be dealing with Jeff on a par—to have him dealing with her as an equal—it was nearly as heady an experience as those more physical ones they'd shared.

Then, from somewhere in the area of the stairs, Lizzie cried. With a look of alarm Geoffrey rose from his chair and headed toward the hall, with Sara close on his heels.

"I'm sorry, Mr. Parker," Caryn apologized quickly. A squirming Lizzie, with her kitten in one arm, put out the other to Geoffrey, who took her readily. "I hope we didn't interrupt your dinner. But she was fussing. I thought I'd take her out for a walk." A pint-size pink parka lay over the nurse's arm.

Geoffrey feigned a frown for the child. "And what's this all about?" he asked in gentle chiding. "Fussing? I thought you were supposed to be sleeping?" He glanced at Caryn. "Did she sleep at all?"

The nurse nodded. "For a few minutes."

The look he favored Lizzie with was decidedly indulgent. "Considering it's a special day, that'll just have to do. How about some dessert?" Turning, he carried her back to the dining room. "Why don't you take some time to yourself, Caryn," he called over his shoulder. "We'll take her out with us for a little while. Plan to be back in time for supper."

"Thank you, Mr. Parker. I'll leave her coat here."

Nodding, Geoffrey turned to Sara. "Does that sound all right to you?"

Given the underlying purpose of the marriage, nothing could have been more appropriate—and appealing. Lizzie looked adorable, peaceful now that she'd found a familiar haven in Geoffrey's arms. Sara knew the feeling but banished it as she reached to smooth down the back of Lizzie's pink corduroy overalls. Even the fleeting touch was a poignant reminder of the child's fragility. It struck a deeply maternal chord.

"Sounds fine," Sara answered with genuine enthusiasm. Then she turned to slip back into her chair. "There's only one problem."

"Oh? What's that?" He'd settled into his own chair, with Lizzie held firmly on his lap.

Her lips curving at the corners, Sara eyed the dessert that, in the interim, Mrs. Fleming had served. One small bite confirmed her suspicion. "Just as I thought. This masterpiece happens to be a very delicious but potent strawberry rum cake. Unless you want a tipsy baby—"

"Mrs. Fleming!"

Within minutes a dish of strawberry ice cream sat beside Geoffrey's rum cake, and he proceeded to direct alternate spoonfuls, one to the child, one to himself. It was a heart-warming sight, suffusing Sara with abundant satisfaction. The two were so obviously pleased with one another. Aside from the occasional glance at Sara and one or two endearing moments when the child held her kitten out in Sara's direction before crushing it back to her chest, Lizzie's attention was solely devoted to Jeff. Indeed, Sara might have felt left out had not Jeff been determined that that shouldn't happen.

"Here," he announced when both plates were empty and he'd finished wiping strawberry dribbles from Lizzie's chin, "why don't you take Lizzie with you while you change. Put on something casual and warm. We'll take a drive and then stop somewhere to walk around. Okay?"

Sara lowered her voice to a near-whisper. "She's apt to be afraid of me, Jeff."

"Nonsense." He looked gently down. "You're not afraid of Sara, are you, Lizzie?" The child looked her way somewhat skeptically. "Of course not! Anyone who makes a special stop for fluffy little kittens can't be all bad." Taking the kitten, he bobbed it against the child's nose. Tickled, she gave a giggle. It was the first time Sara had heard her laugh. The sound was precious.

"There, now." He transferred the child to Sara's arms before either could protest. "She'll be fine sitting on the floor in your room while you change. And then we can go."

He seemed to have it all worked out. But he was a man. What did *he* know! "Uh . . . Jeff?"

"Uh-huh?" He'd already started for the door.

"Shouldn't we bring something with us? I mean, a bottle, a diaper bag, something?" It was the blind leading the blind, though not quite the usual wedding day jitters.

Geoffrey frowned and rubbed the back of his neck. Finally he looked up with a mischievous smile on his face. And that dimple . . .

oh, that dimple. "That sounds great, Sara. I knew I could count on you. In the hall in twenty minutes?" Leaning forward, he popped a kiss on her forehead, then one on the baby's, before vanishing.

Sara stared after him, then stared down at this child who was suddenly in her keeping. The little girl stared back, her eyes wide, her small face registering apprehension. It was enough to jolt Sara to life.

"Well, then," she breathed, holding her warm bundle more comfortably, "it looks like it's you and me, for a couple of minutes at least." Her voice continued in its soft, calming lilt as she slowly walked toward the stairs. "What do you think, Lizzie—shall it be wool slacks or jeans?"

It was wool slacks, in deference to the day's special event. It was also closer to thirty minutes before the two made their way downstairs again. One look at Lizzie's bag on Sara's shoulder and the lightweight snowsuit on Lizzie herself and Geoffrey knew enough not to complain. Further looks at the apparently calm expressions on both the child's face and Sara's and he was privately thrilled. If they were happy that was half the battle.

As it happened, the afternoon was a pleasure all around. Geoffrey took the larger car, safely strapping Lizzie into her seat in back, stowing her stroller in the trunk. After a leisurely drive into the city they parked, then meandered along Pier 39 munching on chocolate chip cookies while admiring shops, street entertainers, even their fellow meanderers. For a mid-November day, the air off the bay was particularly chilly. Sara was glad she'd thought to put the baby in her snowsuit rather than the shorter parka Caryn had left out. Her own hands were cold, much as she tried to warm them in her pockets. When Geoffrey released the stroller handle long enough to snag the hand closest to him and tuck it into his larger pocket, she was grateful. The small gesture warmed her in more ways than one.

They were a family: father, mother, child. Sara couldn't help but stare at their reflection each time they passed a window. It seemed simultaneously real and unreal, so hard to believe yet nearly a fact. Geoffrey pushed the stroller; she kept easy pace close by his side. Lizzie was satisfied to be entertained by the sights around her, looking back only occasionally to assure herself of a familiar face.

"She adores you, Jeff," Sara commented on impulse after one such endearing twist. "I think you've made the right decision to go ahead with the adoption."

"I know I have," he replied quietly. They walked further before Sara ventured to break the companionable silence once more.

"What do you think goes on in that little mind of hers? Do you think she ever expects to see Alex when she looks back at you that way?"

Geoffrey shrugged. "We'll never know for sure. In time she'll forget, although I don't totally want that either. When she's old enough to understand, I want her to know everything possible about Alex and Diane. I may be against her being raised by either of their families, but I certainly want her to come to know them. I don't think they'll argue with that."

"They've been in touch with you, haven't they?"

"Oh, yes." He sighed suggestively.

"Trouble?"

"I'm not sure. They were hesitant when I told them I intended to adopt her."

"Hesitant? You mean negative?"

"They felt that my simply being designated Lizzie's legal guardian would have the same end result." A like thought had crossed Sara's mind, only to be struck from it for the very reason Geoffrey proceeded to voice. "But I want her to have the best of everything. I want her to have *parents*. Not to mention the fact that *I* want *her*."

It was the last thought, tacked on in a lower, more moving tone, that gave Sara pause. It was obvious he did want a child, and that he was eager to devote himself to one. This lovely Sunday afternoon outing seemed to please him as much as it did her. Still, it puzzled her that if he'd wanted a child that badly, he'd not remarried and had one. But then, she reasoned, he now had the best of both worlds. He'd more or less said it once before. He had the joy of the child forever, with the burden of a wife for only a year. One year; then he'd be free to dote on Lizzie to his heart's content.

Feeling momentarily excluded from the twosome's warmth, Sara wondered once again whether things might indeed have been different had they had a child of their own. But no, their marriage had been a horror then, far too rocky to allow for a child. Hard to believe that they were the same couple, walking so peacefully now with this child. Was it the child who brought the peace? Or had the adults simply grown up?

The question returned to her mind with persistent regularity as the afternoon passed. It popped up during the return drive home, resurfaced again during their own light dinner later, seemed to linger prominently when they settled in the downstairs den before a bright birch fire, each in a corner of the plum velour sofa. The distance between them at that moment seemed huge. Had they grown up, or would that distance persist? Was there anything to bring them together?

Sara had only to look at Geoffrey to know the answer to that. She felt it in the sharpening of her senses, the quickening of her pulse. He was as virilely appealing a man as she'd ever seen, and she wanted him.

But his face was drawn, his eyes lost in the hypnotic blaze before them. For all practical purposes she didn't exist. *Practical.* She bandied the word about in her mind as she too stared into the fire. Were warmth and need and caring practical? Was love?

Her serving as Geoffrey's wife for the sake of the adoption proceedings was practical. His offering to help introduce her business to the West Coast was practical. Even their taking little Lizzie for a stroll was in its own way practical.

But what about making love; the ache that

had been slowly building, slowly building all day; the hollow she felt now, that only he could fill? What about that? Where did that fit into Geoffrey's neat little plan?

The hours that passed were filled with inner torment for Sara. She glanced at Jeff; she looked back at the fire. She wanted to speak; she bit her tongue. She stretched her feet toward the fire; she curled them up beneath her. She went through every justification for inching closer to her husband, yet she stayed firmly rooted in her corner.

Through it all Geoffrey sat in a state of complete preoccupation, managing to look distant and divine at the same time. Was that the allure, she wondered, the fact that he seemed unreachable? Or was it the long, strong stretch of legs sheathed in tan corduroy, the magnificence of a torso molded snugly in black wool, the textured hint of a forearm where that sweater was pushed back? Or was it the eyes, dark and brooding; the jaw, firm and straight; the hair, thick and black and falling rakishly forward?

Whatever it was, she found it devastating. When she felt she couldn't bear any more, she struggled at last from her corner. But rather than moving toward Geoffrey, she took a step toward the door.

"I . . . I think I'll go up," she murmured without looking at him. "I'm exhausted." Her bed was waiting in the room she'd used last night, the same one, in the guest wing, in which they'd made such explosive love on the night of the funeral. Though she'd waited all day for his cue, Geoffrey had said nothing about her joining him in the master bedroom.

Perhaps he was waiting for her cue. After all, theirs was a marriage of verbal agreements. But she couldn't speak, couldn't talk of her needs, couldn't beg him for something he might not want. No, she vowed with a sigh as she took another step, then another, as liberated as she'd become over the years, it would still have to be his initiative.

Discouraged, she reached the threshold. Only then did he speak.

Six

"Sara?"

She stopped still, her heart pounding. "Yes?" She didn't turn, simply stood with her head bowed.

"Sara..." His voice was closer this time. She felt his physical presence immediately behind her. Then his hands took her shoulders and turned her gently.

When she met his gaze, it robbed her of breath. His eyes were dark and deep, yet dangerously alight with desire. Did he, too, feel it then? Did he, too, accept the insanity of their being together without... *being* together?

His hands began a gentle caress of her

shoulders while his eyes traced a searing path over the softness of her features. By the time they reached her mouth, Sara felt the heat of him burning into her.

Their lips met at some midway point, touching lightly, then pressing harder, slanting and opening as the kiss deepened, then drawing apart for a gasping breath. For a moment Geoffrey looked angry, as if he was furious at himself for having yielded to her lure. Sara, unable to bear his resentment, reached up to touch his face, to smooth away the marks of his ire.

Oh, yes, he wanted her. She could feel it in the tension of him, in the labored working of his lungs, in the heat of his skin. Coiling her hands around his neck, she stood on tiptoe and brought herself higher, closer. She sampled his lips, nibbling at the lower one until she found the opening she wanted to kiss fully. The tightening of his arms about her back was a victory, as was the feel of his solid length against her.

He was her husband. His lovemaking was her right, her privilege. And she gloried in it. His quiet sigh as he trailed his lips across her cheek and buried them against her neck was sheer heaven. The strength of the hands that caressed her back, that held her up when her knees weakened, was pure bliss.

But what emerged as impassioned ardor to Sara's love-starved heart entailed its share of conflict for Geoffrey. He hadn't planned on doing this. Without love, she'd said. It stung each time he recalled her words. No, he'd promised himself he'd keep his distance, but she was so warm, so attractive, so damn feminine. And she wanted him. She'd left no doubt as to that with her soft urgings. She wanted him. Without love? Was this what she was accustomed to? Had her life without him been dotted with flings for the pure physical satisfaction of it?

In an attempt to regain his senses, he held her back. But her warm brown eyes melted him, and her lips parted in such sweet invitation that he couldn't resist. He was only human, for God's sake! How long could he bear the torment? It had been bad enough thinking of her all week, recalling her body as it had responded to his and anticipating her return. Then today she'd looked beautiful at the wedding, carrying the white rose he'd given her. How he'd like to see her naked carrying that rose.

His arousal heightened part by dream, part by reality, his lips seized hers greedily. He couldn't seem to get enough of her, devouring her tongue and the deepest recesses of her mouth, feeling her response as a hot and fiery thing. Just a little more, he told himself, just a little more . . .

"Take me to bed," Sara whispered, finally abandoning all hesitancy to yield to the burning need within. "Please, Jeff. I want you so . . ." Her words trailed off against the line of his jaw. She felt him stiffen but was too emotionally tangled to think anything of it beyond a taut-held control.

It was that, too. At her soft, soulful plea, Geoffrey would have gladly taken her there and then, with the velour sofa as their bed and the crackling fire as an erotic accompaniment. Without love? Did he want that? Lord only knew he'd had his fill of empty encounters over the years. Could this be empty with Sara? Maybe on her part—after all, he'd all but bribed her to marry him.

But his body was against any lofty sights he might have held. If she wanted him, he wanted her no less. Perhaps if he simply touched her, tested her warmth a little longer . . .

She made no protest when he slipped his

hand beneath her knees and lifted her. With her arms wrapped tightly around his neck, she buried her face against its warm column and inhaled his musky scent. He was all man. Her body tingled with this knowledge as he carried her down the hall and up the stairs. Her eyes closed, she let her senses savor the anticipation. His footsteps were firm and sure. She trusted him. It wasn't until he'd laid her gently on the bed and reached to switch on the lamp that she realized where she was: not his room but hers. She looked up at him questioningly when he came to lean over her.

Arms straightened and propped on fists, he held himself away as long as he could. He'd kiss her again, he decided—one long, lingering kiss—and then he'd leave her to her loveless dreams. But as he lowered his head, she reached for him, and, responding against his better judgment, he found himself sitting on the bed, cradling her pliant body. Her lips were so very soft, answering his every move with one of their own. One kiss. He'd let it drag on a little longer . . .

To Sara the moment was exquisite. The tension in Jeff only enhanced her excitement, in turn eliciting even greater response from him. When his arms began a restless roving of her back, she arched closer, seeking the same heightened contact he did. Their bodies were well in tune, harmonizing ecstatically. Her hands defined the manly swell of his shoulders; his hands ran along her sides from hip to arm. And all the while their lips clung with strange desperation.

One kiss, and to touch her for a minute—that was all he wanted. Lowering her slowly to the bed, Geoffrey framed her face with his hands, then drew them down the graceful line of her neck to her throat. He could feel the rapid thud of her heart, see in her face the level of arousal to which he'd driven her. His upper arms bore the brand of her whitened fingers, while his own worked one after the other on the buttons of her blouse. He kissed her again one more time as he spread the fine fabric, then drew back to look at her.

"Oh, Sara," he breathed hoarsely. His hands moved over her, shaping her breasts to his palms. The lace of her bra was as delicate as she, its silken cup nearly as smooth as her skin. Leaning forward, he touched his lips to those upper curves. Her swelling urged him on, as did her throaty words of desire.

"That's it, Jeff . . . yes . . ." Threading her fingers through his hair, she held him even closer. At that moment they were well and truly married. Anything and everything of hers she wanted him to have. That it happened to be her body mattered little. The joy was in the giving, wholly and irrevocably.

Feeling himself beginning to lose control, Geoffrey tried to pull back. But his bodily impulses easily overpowered those from his brain. His lips only moved lower, hungering for the softness of her breast. And then there were her hands, slipping seductively beneath his sweater. His skin burned at her touch. Helplessly he yearned for more; indulgently he granted himself another minute.

Sara gasped in excitement when he deftly unhooked her bra. She felt the coolness of the air, then an incredible warmth with the return of his hands to her body. His fingers traced her fullness, rounding her breasts and moving in gently exploratory circles, each smaller than the one before, each moving closer to the erotic touchpoint of her nipple.

"Please . . ." She gave an urgent whisper and was rewarded when the firm pads of his thumbs stroked those hardened points. She bit her lip at the current that surged through her, closing her eyes at the intensity, clasping his arms all the harder. His muscles flexed at her touch, but she barely knew that. Nor did she see the shadow of anxiety cross his face.

Enough, he told himself, but his hands continued their intimate caress, seeming magnetically drawn to her ivory flesh. Leaning forward, he kissed one nipple lightly . . . just once . . . but it was only a crumb to a man starving for this particular sweet. Another kiss. He moved his tongue over the pebbled peak. He opened his mouth and took it in fully. How could he possibly stop when she cried so softly to him to go on?

And he wanted more, as did she. With a gentle nudge she urged him back, sitting up before him to tug off his black sweater. Beneath it, the firmness of his chest was warm and waiting. She touched it in wonder and felt him shudder.

"Sara . . ." he rasped in warning, but the warning was self-directed. His entire body felt afire. Before long he'd be unable to think of anything beyond burying himself in her once more. "Sara, no . . ." Taking her wrists, he forced her hands from his chest. "That's enough."

Her eyes widened in alarm, her voice little more than a ragged rasp. "What's wrong, Jeff?"

"This isn't what I intended when I asked you to marry me."

"What?" Surfacing from the hazy realm of passion, she couldn't seem to understand him.

He gritted his teeth, as much against the lure of her helplessness as against his own frustration. "I said that this has gone far enough." She continued to stare uncomprehendingly. "We've got to stop."

"You're my husband, Jeff!"

"On paper—and for the benefit of the courts. We made a deal. You get your West Coast branch, I get a wife for a year." He spoke quickly, drumming the thoughts into his own head. "Outward appearances are the important thing. I didn't bargain on . . . this." What he hadn't bargained on was wanting her as badly as he did. In truth, he was amazed he'd been able to stop when he had.

"But you were the one who talked about how good it was—"

"And *you* talked about how phony it would be," he spat back.

"Jeff . . ." she tried to protest, but he released her wrists and stood, in complete control of himself at last.

"No, Sara." The set of his jaw brooked no argument. "You were right. I can wait. Besides, you've got a very early plane to catch. I think you'd better get what sleep you can. You have a long trip in front of you." Snatching up his sweater, he turned his back on her, leaving only a broad expanse of tanned flesh to her view, then nothing at all.

With the slamming of the door she began to tremble in a way that had nothing to do with passion and everything to do with despair. Her own words, cried out in a moment of weakness, had come back to haunt her. It was small solace that he seemed bent on respecting her claim that without love, the act of making love would be empty. It was small solace when she loved him so. She always had; she always would. She'd loved him from that first week in Snowmass, even through the two downhill years of their marriage, yes, even through eight years of separation. Why else would she have agreed to his second marriage proposal but to be with him?

Without love, the act of making love would be phony. But she'd been referring to *him!* He was the one whose emotional involvement fell short, not her!

He could wait, he'd just said. Wait—until the year was up and he was free to satisfy his ache with another? For he'd wanted her. She was sure of that. And she could satisfy him; of that, too, she was sure. But a year of frustration? Was that what he'd bargained for? Was that what *she* faced?

It was as she'd feared on the night of the funeral. One reminder of how well their bodies meshed and she wanted him again. And it would continue, as it had so many years before. Six months after their original marriage, she'd known it was doomed. But she'd stuck it out. Why? Because she'd loved him and had been unable to bear the thought of letting him go. Her eventual decision to leave had been made only when the marriage itself had become unbearable, when she'd come to the realization that if she was to survive as a human being, she needed to shed the Parker cloak.

Now, though, the situation was different. She was a human being with an independent life. Yet she'd promised him a year—indeed, she wanted that year. But was there hope? Could she dare to wonder whether it might be possible to capture what they'd had once in a private bungalow in Snowmass? She didn't know. She just didn't know!

The night brought little sleep and even fewer answers. When she finally dragged herself from bed Monday morning, she was glad to be done with the endless equivocating. What she didn't count on was the tug at her heart when she gently kissed Lizzie good-bye, or the pregnant silence that permeated Geoffrey's small car during the drive to the airport. Having left all but her handbag behind at the house, she again protested that he needn't wait with her. Again he overruled her. This time, though, there seemed a reason for his wait. With a hand lightly at her back, he guided her to a pair of chairs away from the central gathering of travelers. Once she was comfortably seated, he slid down beside her. When he finally spoke, low and for her ears alone, she wasn't surprised at his choice of subject.

"Sara, about last night—"

"Please, Jeff. Let's just forget it." She'd had enough of brooding. Somewhere in the middle of the night she'd lost her perspective.

He faced her. "I can't do that, and I doubt you can either." Of course, he was right. She listened more patiently. "I'm trying to make things easier for both of us, Sara." Even to him it sounded absurd, given the frustration he felt just now. But he'd given it agonizing hours of thought. "We've got a year together. After that we'll go our separate ways. As I see it, we'd be smart to minimize our involvement—"

Once again Sara interrupted him. "But how can we do that? I mean, marriage *is* a commitment. It *is* involvement, whether we want that or not. I tried to tell you last week—"

"And I tried to tell you that this isn't an ordinary marriage. We've got a bargain." He rubbed his thumb against those other clenched fingers. "As it is, I'll have a problem on my hands when Lizzie gets attached to you and then you take off."

Sara stared, hearing an accusation she couldn't fathom. "Like I did before? Is that what you're saying?"

He shifted his sights to the approaching airline personnel and sighed. "If it sounded that way, I apologize. I was angry when you left me before. But you were right to have done it. I can see that now." The admission seemed to be a hard-wrung one. He twisted his head to eye her once more. "If you'd stayed with me, you would never have become the person you are now."

"At least we agree on that," she murmured grudgingly.

Geoffrey sat back, obviously tired. "Look, I

really don't want to fight about this. All I want is to make the year bearable—"

A sharp pain around her heart brought Sara to her feet. "I've got to run. They're starting to board now. Good-bye, Jeff."

"Sara—" He was on his feet beside her, but she whirled and headed for the gate at a steady clip. "Sara!" he called a final time, but she refused to acknowledge him. The last thing she wanted was for him to see the tears in her eyes, to see how much he'd hurt her.

It seemed forever that she stood in line with her ticket in her hand, praying that Geoffrey would stay away. She bit her lip and swallowed hard. She tried to think of something, anything, that might keep those tears from overflowing. When at last she found herself on board the plane in a window seat facing the terminal, she pressed her hand to her upper lip and looked back. But her vision was blurred, too blurred to detect the tall, dark figure standing there wondering at the pain he'd seen in her eyes before she'd fled.

He was still wondering on Thursday morning as he stood in the same spot awaiting her arrival. He'd worried about her since Monday, had even called this time to make sure she hadn't changed her plans. The conversation might as well have been recorded, he could remember every word so well.

The phone had rung five times before she'd picked it up.

"Sara . . . ?"

There had been a pause, then a soft, "Yes?"

"It's Jeff. Am I disturbing you?" He'd timed the call to make it evening in New York, that limbo time between work and bed.

"No, no," she'd answered gently. "I was just finishing up some designs for a show we're doing in January."

"A show?"

"It's a benefit, actually. I'm providing the jewelry to accessorize the fashions. One of the pieces will be raffled off. The rest will go on to be part of Bendel's collection."

"Sounds good." What sounded really good was the fact that she seemed to be looking beyond whatever it was that had hurt her when last they'd been together. He hesitated, his voice growing deeper. "How are you?"

"Fine. Busy." Again she spoke more softly. "And you?"

"The same." Busy, yes. Fine, questionable. But what harm was there in a little white lie?

"Is Lizzie all right?"

"She's fine." He couldn't help but smile. "Adorable. Crawling all over the place, standing up whenever she can. It's so cute to see. She walks along holding to the furniture but can't quite take that first step without sitting down hard."

Sara had chuckled, sharing his appreciation of the vision. "It's about that time, isn't it? When *do* children start to walk?"

"The pediatrician says it could be any time now."

"Have *you* spoken to him?"

"I took Lizzie to see *her* yesterday."

Sara had laughed again, and he'd felt much better. "Sorry about that. I guess I've got my own stereotypes to overcome."

"No problem. She really is a nice woman."

"Young and smashing?"

"Married and a mother herself."

Was that a sigh of relief he'd heard? She'd gone on so quickly he hadn't known for sure. "Sounds eminently qualified. Does Lizzie like her?"

"Hates her. Screams every time the woman walks into the room."

"Oh, no! Why?"

He'd cleared his throat in good humor. "I think it has something to do with inoculations—you know, measles, mumps, DPT-type thing."

"Ahhhhh. That'll do it every time." They'd both laughed then, and Geoffrey had felt like a million. But Sara had continued on a more quiet note. "She's got a birthday coming up, doesn't she?"

"December eleventh."

"One year old. That's quite a milestone. We'll have to have a celebration. I'm sure Alex and Diane would have—" She'd cut herself off abruptly.

"That's all right, Sara. I've been thinking the same thing myself. Alex and Diane certainly would have made a big thing of her birthday. I want her to have no less."

"She will," Sara'd said, then added a pensive "Jeff?"

"Yes?"

"Is your lawyer working on the adoption?"

He'd nodded, forgetting she couldn't see him, trying in vain to analyze the hesitancy in her voice. "He'll bring the preliminary papers over for us to sign on Friday. Sound all right?"

"That's fine." For a moment then there had been silence. "Have you . . . have you told people, Jeff?"

He'd known instantly what she'd meant. "About us? Yes."

"What—what did they say?" she'd asked in a near-whisper, surprising him with her trepidation. He'd thought her so self-assured now. Was there a trace of that old insecurity left?

"They were really pleased for us," he'd answered boldly, wanting nothing more than to bolster her strength. Strange, but he was fast getting used to this new, more confident woman.

"I'm glad."

"How about you, Sara? They saw the ring, didn't they?"

His was a reference to a conversation they'd had the weekend before. Sara followed it easily, a smile shaping her words. "Yes, they saw the ring."

"Well, what did they say?"

She'd laughed softly. "You don't really want to know."

"I do." He was so thoroughly enjoying the ease of their discussion that he felt able to take anything. "Tell me."

Her voice held a humor that softened her words. "They said, 'You're *what?*' Sound familiar?"

He'd nodded. "My mother."

"Right."

"Were they displeased?" It was his turn to sound hesitant. The last thing he needed was for her people to be against him. Had the tables turned so completely?

"Not displeased so much as stunned. They'd pretty much assumed I wasn't interested in marriage."

"And of course you told them how wrong they were."

"Of course."

"Did they finally come around?"

She'd purposely kept him dangling then with those few seconds' silence; he was sure of it. But he could feel no ill will toward her. She deserved the moment after all she'd suffered once.

"Oh, yes"—she'd given a bounteous sigh—"they came around. It helped when I explained—shyly, of course—that we'd been married before. The suddenness became less of an issue. But then, they *had* to come around. They had no choice. I'm the boss."

"It helps."

"So I've learned."

"But what about the—others?"

"Oh, you mean my friends, as opposed to business associates?"

"Yes." He'd had to struggle to keep his tone even. "Those ones who escort you to all your fancy balls and things."

"There aren't all *that* many," she'd chided, but he'd come back quickly.

"Fancy balls . . . or men?"

"*Either!*" Her declaration had rung loudly from coast to coast.

"Then let's consider the men. Have you told them you're no longer available?"

"You mean," she rejoined sweetly, "have I called each one just to tell him he's no longer in the running? No."

"No? Why not? Sara, I told you that I'll be your—" Even now, he recalled how quick he'd been to get angry, though her subsequent reasoning had been correct.

"Calm down, Jeff, and listen to me. I'm not about to sit with a list of friends and acquaintances and systematically phone them to tell them I've gotten married on the spur of the moment." For the first time her voice had hardened. "It's no big thing. Only for a year—which I certainly couldn't tell them." Just when he had begun to stiffen, she'd taken a breath and continued more gently. "Of course I've called my closest friends, male and female. And I was supposed to go to the theater this weekend with a fellow; I told him the truth when I canceled the date. In time they'll all know. Word spreads—or hadn't you known?"

He'd known, all right. How could he have helped but know, given the number of calls he'd received that week from one person or another who'd heard the news. It had all culminated in the party planned for Saturday night; but he hadn't told her that on the phone. Hadn't quite had the courage. Besides, there had been other things to discuss.

"Well, that's taken care of then." He'd been pleased enough with her answer. "By the way, the workmen are really moving it at the cottage."

"They are?" she'd asked excitedly. "Are they having any trouble deciphering my plans?"

It had been his turn to chuckle. "They did say something about your sketches being a deviation from those of the normal architect."

"I can put my man on it if they want. He did a great job for us here. I had just wanted to get something done quickly for your men—"

"It's fine, Sara. They're accommodating

guys. You'll be amazed when you see the progress. The place has been gutted and they're doing the lighting—"

"Gutted? I didn't want them to go to all that trouble. A simple little renovation work would have been fine. Maybe I *should* get Harris to draw up something more detailed!"

"Sara, *it's fine!*" He'd calmed her, enjoying the role of the rock. "I'll tell you what. Why don't you give me the name and number of your architect and I'll have the contractor speak with him. You'll be able to speak with the contractor yourself on Friday. He'll be working."

"Oh, Jeff, speaking of Friday, I've been making calls and going over samples. The first of the deliveries will be made then. I—I hope you don't mind."

"Mind? Of course not. I told you to do whatever you wanted with the cottage."

Again she'd grown more hesitant, almost apologetic. "It's not for the cottage. It's . . . for Lizzie's room."

It had taken him several seconds to follow. When he had, he'd been amazed. "Lizzie's . . . oh, *Lizzie's* room. You've been doing things from there?"

"I said I would."

"But you've got so much else to do."

"This is just as important. And it's really easy. There are people here I've worked with—wallpaper, carpeting, that type of thing. They've all been so excited." As was she. It had come through the phone wire loud and clear. "I found the perfect wallpaper—it's red and white and yellow, bright and shiny . . . but maybe you want to see it first?"

Having enjoyed her enthusiasm, Geoffrey reacted swiftly to staunch her sudden caution. "No, Sara," he'd replied with confidence, "I trust your judgment. You pick out what you think is right for her and then I'll be as surprised as she is when it comes."

"That's the point. It's coming Friday."

"How did you ever manage that? I mean, I always thought it took time to order things like wallpaper."

Sara's voice had been filled with pride. "The people I'm using are wonderful. When I explained the situation, they got right on the phone to contacts of theirs in the bay area. The carpeting is coming from L.A., but the rest of it is more local."

"The rest of it?" he'd asked. Even now he

half-envisioned an army of interior decorators descending on the house with bolts of material trailing off every which way.

"You'll see," she'd said pertly, then promptly changed the subject. "Jeff?"

"Hmmm?"

"Is everything set for tomorrow?"

"Uh-huh. It'll be quiet. Just the three of us."

"Gordie's not coming?"

Even now Geoffrey marveled that Sara should want to see his younger brother. Gordon had been one of the many who'd made her erstwhile stint here unpleasant. "No, not this year."

"You told him, didn't you?"

"Uh, yes. He ... didn't take it very well." But then Gordie had always begrudged what Geoffrey had done. The first time around he'd viewed Sara as a fortune hunter. This time he'd been more generous. He'd merely suggested that Jeff had gone soft.

"Oh, dear," she'd mused softly.

"What about your family, Sara? Have you broken the news to them?"

She'd been quiet for a time before she'd answered. "Uh, no. I, uh, I . . . I didn't have the guts. Maybe if I get brave I'll give them a call over the weekend."

Given what he'd so recently learned, Geoffrey hadn't been able to blame her. "That would be nice, especially since it's the holiday. But only if you feel comfortable. I'd like it to be an enjoyable weekend. Sara?" He recalled faltering, then forging on before he'd lost his courage. "I'm sorry if I upset you Monday morning." It had been weighing on his mind all week, that pained look he'd seen.

Her voice had spanned the distance more softly. "It's all right. I was tired. Not my usual self."

"Still, I want things to be right between us."

"So do I," she'd offered, in such a wistful half-whisper that he'd almost believed they were talking of the same thing.

"Then . . . I'll see you in the morning?"

Although he'd expected a simple yes, he'd received an addendum to the conversation. If he'd let his imagination roam free, he might have believed that she'd been purposely prolonging their talk.

"I'm sorry I couldn't get out today, but the holiday flights have been booked for months. It was only a favor that got me the seat in the morning."

"Another friend?" It shouldn't have been any surprise to him. He could easily understand how she would attract hordes of admirers. Like Mrs. Fleming. She hadn't stopped raving about "the new Mrs.," as she called Sara. Sophisticated, but without airs; that was what she'd said. It seemed that the breakfast in the kitchen had impressed her no end.

"Yes, another friend." Sara had seemed to smile into the phone. "She works for the airline."

"Then please thank her, for all of us."

"I will."

"Till tomorrow?"

"Right."

"Sleep well."

"You too."

Stirring from the window now as her plane touched down, Geoffrey relived that warm, cozy feeling the phone call had inspired. They'd gotten along so well long distance. Was it the safety valve of separation, or simply the old adage that distance made the heart grow fonder? He *was* looking forward to seeing her, more than he'd like to admit. And yes, he had slept well last night. Better than he'd slept in a while.

This time Sara was among the first swarm of passengers to deplane. She'd chosen her seat purposely, feeling incredibly impatient, excited even in spite of the week's torment. When she caught sight of Geoffrey's dark head, her pulse skipped a beat. When her eyes met his, it raced onward. But when she found herself face to face with him at last, she was momentarily tongue-tied. Fortunately he was in better control.

Gently grasping her arms, he stood for a minute smiling down at her. "Hi."

She struggled to mouth a return "Hi." It was tough, what with that deep, deep sound of his voice, the distraction of his luring gaze and the dimple that beamed at her from his right cheek—not to mention the subtle movement of his fingers on the Harris tweed of her blazer.

"How was the trip?"

"Great," she breathed airily.

"You were right on time."

"It was a smooth flight."

His smile persisted, as did hers. "Happy Thanksgiving, Sara."

"You too, Jeff."

He stared at her a moment longer, then looked around the room. "Should we give them a show?"

Unable to take her eyes from him, she simply asked, "Who?"

He jerked his chin in a semicircle at the people around them. "Anyone who's watching. After all"—he leaned closer, his voice a velvet caress—"we're supposed to be married."

"So we are," she whispered, her lips parting to meet his. She felt his hands tighten on her arms, felt her own slip beneath his jacket and around his back. But above all she felt the warm hello of his kiss and answered it easily. When he drew back at last, she felt bereft, but only until he threw an arm across her shoulders and drew her into step beside him.

"Luggage?" he asked softly. She shook her head. "Good. Let's go."

And so they headed home in an atmosphere of goodwill that was startlingly different from the week of anguish Sara had endured. As many times as she had replayed his words— "All I want is to make the year bearable"—she ached. It hadn't only been the words; it had been his tone of voice as well. Resignation, fatigue, indifference—what did it matter? One was as diametrically opposed to her feeling of love as the other.

Having not permitted herself to hope, she'd been surprised when he'd called. Pleasantly surprised. Delightfully surprised. Oh, yes, she told herself, he had simply felt bad that he'd been so blunt. But the fact that he'd made the effort was . . . something. And now, with a kiss at the airport and gentle looks here and there as he drove, she felt newly optimistic. It was a long holiday weekend and she was determined to enjoy it. Hell, where *else* would she be if not here with Jeff?

"What would you have done for Thanksgiving if all this hadn't happened?" Geoffrey echoed her thoughts as he drove.

"Oh, I don't know. I probably would have spent the day with friends. There are lots of us displaced souls in Manhattan, so it's easy enough to find company."

"You never go home?"

"I have, once or twice." She cast a distant look out the window. "But when things are so busy it's hard to get out there."

"You got here," he chided.

Her head shot back. "This is different!" Then she paused, looked down, fidgeted with the gold band on her finger before looking outside again. "I suppose you're right. I could go to see them more. But I feel awkward. It's as though my leaving Des Moines ten years ago was an irreparable break. I send them letters pretty often. Somehow it's easier on paper." There seemed no point in elaborating on her attempts to send her parents money. Their stubborn pride was her problem, not his.

"Do you see your brothers and sisters at all?"

She shook her head. "Not often. Once in a while one of them passes through New York and we'll meet for lunch or dinner. I love seeing them, but they have their own lives."

Geoffrey's voice lowered then. "You must miss them."

"I do," she said without a second thought. "We were close as kids. There's nothing like a crisis to bring a family together, and we lived a steady crisis for years." She sighed. "But things are pretty quiet there now. My father is retired and we're all out on our own. I do miss them, though."

"Then," he interjected on a lighter note, "we'll just have to keep you busy enough over the weekend to keep you from getting melancholy."

That was precisely what he did—he and Lizzie. Caryn had been given the holiday off and wasn't due back until Saturday, leaving Mrs. Fleming to cover until Geoffrey and Sara returned, at which point the two could take over as full-time mother and father.

It began with a turkey dinner late Thursday

afternoon, with Lizzie in her high chair eating child-size bites of just about everything they did. It continued with a tour of the cottage, a brainstorming session on the best setup for Sara's workshop, a prolonged play-and-bath session with Lizzie. To Sara's surprise, Geoffrey was as handy with a diaper as he was knowledgeable as to the whereabouts of baby powder, tiny nightgowns and hairbrushes.

"You're very good," she complimented him in good humor. "I'm really feeling like the novice here."

"I've had more practice lately," he explained as he drew the brush gently through wisps of fine golden hair.

"You must be busy, coming home from work to take care of Lizzie, taking her to the doctor and all. Where do you find the time to do everything?"

His glance held mock punishment. "For a liberated woman, you're really unliberated. What I'm doing is no different from what any other working parent does. If something means enough to you, you find time to do it."

Sara would have pondered his words and their pointedness had not Jeff abruptly dropped the discussion. Sitting Lizzie up on the dressing table, he examined his handiwork with a satisfied smile. She promptly grabbed onto the fabric of his shirt and pulled herself to her feet, joining the dialogue with a buoyant stream of syllables that to everyone but herself were meaningless. "You don't say," Geoffrey teased her, falling into the game. "Tell me something I *don't* know."

When the child proceeded to do just that, Sara couldn't help but laugh. "She looks as if she knows just what she's saying. If only we could understand her."

"The sounds are there. She's just got to get them in the right order. Here, Lizzie." He reached for the rubber turtle she'd carried with her from the tub and held it before her enticingly. "Tur-tle. Can you say that? Tur-tle."

The little girl eagerly reached for her toy. "T-t-t-t-t . . ."

"Atta girl! How about this." He knelt to pick up a bright fabric ball. "Ball. B-b-ball."

When Lizzie waved the turtle in the air with a pleased "T-t-t-t-t . . ." Sara broke up completely. But Jeff was undaunted. Before she knew what was happening, he threw his free arm around her shoulder, hugged her close to his side and gently poked her ribs. But his eyes were on Lizzie. "Sa-ra," he enunciated slowly. "Sa-ra."

Lizzie looked at Sara, grinned and offered a speech filled with ba-ba-ba-bas, pranced for a second on the table before falling back on her bottom. When her little lip quivered, Sara quickly reached for her and took her into her arms.

"That's all right, sweetie," she crooned, pressing the child to her as she turned and walked toward the rocker. "You'll make it one of these days. We all did." Settling into the chair, she gently rocked back and forth, as hypnotized by the sweet baby smell of the child in her arms as by the warmth of the little one herself. Lizzie lay contentedly for several minutes, then bobbed her head up and proudly produced the handful of hair she'd discovered on Sara's shoulder. When she pulled, Sara feigned intense pain. "Easy does it. That's attached, you know."

The child grinned, tugged several more times, then offered a soft "Sa-sa-sa-sa . . ." as a consolation prize. Sara was fully satisfied.

She also was exhausted. By the time ten o'clock rolled around, after a comfortable evening playing backgammon with Jeff, she excused herself and headed for her room. Jeff made no move to follow, for which she was actually glad. The day had been lovely. But much as she would have liked nothing more than to spend the night in his arms, she wouldn't have pushed the issue for anything. They'd managed to arrive at a temporary truce. She was happy to let it stand.

As it happened, it was lucky she got the sleep that she had. For Friday was hectic, with deliveries of carpeting, wallpaper, lights and furniture, workmen to be directed from the house to the cottage and back and Lizzie perched on her hip through it all.

"Why don't you leave the little one with me," Mrs. Fleming had suggested when it appeared that everything was going to happen at once, with Geoffrey away at his office.

But Sara had been vehement. "If you can just have one of the fellows move her old crib into another room—why don't you make it mine—so she can nap a little later, we'll be fine. As long as she's occupied watching the work, I can supervise it."

And it had been surprisingly easy. Lizzie was perfectly happy being held, Sara perfectly happy inquiring, directing and suggesting. It was only later in the day that exhaustion hit them both. When Geoffrey finally returned late in the afternoon, both of his women were sound asleep, Lizzie in her crib, Sara on her nearby bed. He stood for long moments savoring the sight, then sat down beside Sara and gently kissed her cheek. She awoke instantly, bolting to a sitting position, feeling infinitely irresponsible.

"I'm sorry, Jeff," she whispered, looking quickly over at Lizzie to make sure she was all right. "I hadn't expected to fall asleep. I thought I'd just lie down and keep an eye on her—" Geoffrey cut her off with a sound kiss that left them both breathless. "What was *that* for?" she gasped at last, pleased if puzzled.

"That," he whispered hoarsely, "was for being as irresistibly appealing as"—he cocked his head toward the baby—"she is." Then he leaned forward and took her lips more gently, more persuasively, more seductively.

"And that?" she somehow managed to ask when her lips were free at last.

"That is for everything else you've got that she hasn't . . . yet."

"Flattery will get you everywhere."

"Oh?" The twinkle in his eyes set her pulse to tripping. "Then if I tell you how very beautiful and bright and enterprising you are, will you . . . agree to go with me to a party at the Shipleys' tomorrow night?"

Seven

He held his breath, all humor gone. She had always hated parties. She had always hated his crowd. But these *were* his friends and their intentions were good. If only she would give it another chance.

"That would be lovely," she said, and smiled up at him. "What's the occasion?"

He was stunned. "Uh..." He cleared his throat. "When John heard that we were married, he decided a celebration was in order." He hesitated. "You remember John and Rebecca, don't you?"

"How could I forget?" She winced, but there was a very definite element of amusement in her tone. "They have a magnificent old house with a very lovely back patio—which is where I used to retreat to study the moon by my lonesome. It was dark and private, nearly beyond detection."

"Sara, you didn't . . ."

"Where did you think I was?" She feigned hurt. "Or didn't you even miss me?"

Geoffrey chose not to answer, on that score at least. "You won't be able to do it this time."

"You're right. It'd be pretty chilly out there this time of year."

"That wasn't what I meant—"

"Shhh! You'll wake the baby."

His eyes narrowed on her smug smile. "You're enjoying this, aren't you?" She was, and he couldn't quite understand it. He'd expected some reluctance, some hesitancy on her part. Yet she seemed the image of contentment. On top of which, wearing jeans and a heavy-knit turtleneck sweater, she looked very, very sexy. With her hair flowing free, messed just enough, and that lingering drop of sleep in her eyes . . .

She saw it coming and put out a hand, but her palm simply flattened on his chest when he backed her down to the bed. "Jeff, the baby!"

"She's sleeping. We'll be quiet."

"What do you mean, we'll be quiet?"

"Just a kiss or two. No noise."

"But Jeff—" Again he cut her off, again with his lips. And there was nothing for her to do but enjoy it, which she did with total relish. The baby was their chaperon, albeit a sleeping one. Her silent presence was reminder enough of the purpose of their marriage.

But could a child really compete with the lure of a big, handsome man for a woman's attentions, particularly when the child was sleeping and the man was wide awake and willing? And when his lips caressed hers with such swift seduction, she was helpless to do anything other than be the woman of passion he inspired.

"Mmmm. Your lips are always so sweet," he whispered, but gave her no time to answer, for he took them again with a mounting hunger that left no doubt as to his taste.

Sara reeled beneath the onslaught, wanting to push him back, unable to do anything but slide her hands around him and urge him closer. The weight of his body pressing her down was a stimulant in itself, as was the growing urgency she felt in him. She let her fingers explore the strength of the muscles beneath his shirt, then slipped them forward again to his chest when he arched away.

His eyes drank greedily of her love-flushed face, and his voice was thick and low. "How can you have spent the day with Lizzie and the workmen and still come out looking like this?"

"I'm a mess!"

"A pretty sexy one, then. *Damn.*" He cursed and kissed her hard. Rolling half to his side, he splayed his fingers across her thigh and slowly inched them upward. Sara felt a simultaneous heat rising, rising beneath the gentle pressure of his hand from her thigh to her stomach, across her waist to her middle, then further, over the aching swell of her breast to her neck. Unable to take the torment of frustration, she grabbed his hand and stayed it beneath her chin. With a soft kiss to his palm, she looked up at him.

"Please, Jeff. No more. I can't take it."

"*You* can't take it?" he rasped, then caught himself as if surprised at his outburst, slowly sat up on the edge of the bed and made to straighten his tie before thinking again and taking it off. He looked back at her once in confusion, glanced down at the rug as he absently fingered the tie, then looked back at her again. "But you will go to the party with me, won't you?"

Sara felt as though she'd missed a beat. At times Geoffrey confused her so. Now, for example, that war between passion and constraint—she knew that he wanted her yet he could turn off on command. Was that the way it was when the heart was uninvolved? But then they'd gotten along so well since she'd arrived. Was he totally uninvolved, or was it the fact of a growing involvement that he resented?

To these questions she had no answers. Regarding his question, the situation was different. "Of course I'll go to the party," she responded gently. "It should be lovely."

If Geoffrey was stunned by the utter calm with which she'd accepted the invitation, he was further astounded by her absolute poise throughout the event itself. Nor were there signs of the jitters beforehand. She was good-humored through Saturday morning, buoyant through Saturday afternoon and uncompromisingly self-assured when she later descended the stairs wearing a long gown of black satin with white trim at the neck, waist and wrists adding a look of tasteful chic.

"Very nice," he complimented, his eyes compensating for the understatement with a deep gray glitter of appreciation.

"You too," she returned with due awareness of his black dress suit and crisp white shirt and the way they hugged the long, lean lines of his body. As she approached she noted the lingering dampness of his hair, the ultrasmoothness of his jaw, the barest hint of subtle aftershave, all of which further enhanced the image of exultant masculinity with which she would have to deal.

She'd barely begun to regain control of her pulse when he reached to touch the creation of ivory and gold at her ear. "They're beautiful, Sara. They suit the dress—and you—perfectly."

Seeking her wrist, she fingered the matching bracelet. "I designed them for a show last spring, then fell in love with the dress and had to have the whole outfit." She gave a sheepish grin. "I feel very, very elegant in them."

For a second—just a second—Geoffrey recalled the girl-woman she'd been when he'd first met her. Then she'd been cowed by the wardrobe he'd insisted on buying her and had worn each dressy piece as if a wrinkle would ruin it. Now, in a gown every bit as sensitive, she seemed totally at ease and, yes, elegant.

He was but one of many who thought as much that night. When they arrived at the Shipleys', they were greeted with enthusiastic curiosity. Just as Sara remembered many of those present, they remembered her—and were not quite sure what they would find. As the evening progressed, however, curiosity gave way to unabashed surprise which, in turn, wound up on a final note of awe. Sara McCray Parker, this second time around, took Geoffrey's San Francisco set by storm.

Knowing his friends as he did, Geoffrey could see it clearly. Though he didn't leave Sara's side long enough to allow for any man-to-man discussions, he read those looks well and felt tremendous pride.

Sara thrived. The fact that she held his hand or his arm—or was it he who held her? Neither knew for sure—throughout the evening was secondary to her display of social grace among his friends. The fact that these were the same people who had once intimidated her so thoroughly continued to amaze him.

"Sara, you remember the Monacos—Dan and Cheryl—don't you?"

"Of course." She smiled graciously and extended her hand in turn to each half of the stylishly dressed couple. Dan and Cheryl had been members of the country club where she'd suffered any number of golfing nightmares. "How are you, Dan? Cheryl, it's good to see you."

"Our pleasure," said the first.

"And congratulations," added his mate. "But I have to tell you how pleased I am to hear the news. I have a friend in New York who's been raving about your things! And now you're planning on selling your work here?"

Sara leaned back toward Jeff just enough to feel the warmth of his hand at her waist. "The headquarters will remain in New York. But Jeff has convinced me that a branch on the West Coast would be a success."

"For you, perhaps," Dan teased. "As for me, I wonder. My wife can be a spender when she gets going."

Threading a crepe-sheathed arm through his, Cheryl crinkled up her nose. "Don't pay any attention to him, Sara. I think it's fantastic. Your jewelry is smashing." She eyed the earrings. "These *are* yours, aren't they?"

"They are," Geoffrey interjected far more boldly than Sara would have done.

"Jeff, Sara . . ." Their host approached with another guest in tow. Geoffrey was quick to do the honors.

"Good to see you, Stu." He shook hands with the newcomer, then turned to Sara. "You remember the senator, honey, don't you?"

Swept up in the game of playing lovers, Sara savored Jeff's endearment even as she turned to the gray-haired, debonair Stuart Javnowski. "Senator, it's good to see you."

"The pleasure is mine, Sara." His puzzlement would have been humorous had not Sara been cognizant of its cause. "It's been quite a while."

"That it has. You're still keeping things moving in Sacramento?"

The older man chuckled. "Me and a whole crew of others. Now if we were only on the same side of issues . . ."

"You'd be bored to tears," Geoffrey teased. "Without the fighting, what fun would it be?" When the senator simply cocked a brow, Geoffrey grew more serious. "How's Ellen feeling?" Turning, he explained to Sara. "She was operated on several weeks ago."

"Nothing serious," the senator waffled in vague explanation. "But she's still weak and tired or she'd have been here tonight. She sends her congratulations, though."

"Geoffrey!" All eyes shifted to the woman who approached. "What's this I hear about your marrying?"

"Sara, I don't believe you know Danielle Howard. Danielle, my wife, Sara."

Sara found herself face to face with a beauty of a woman, a woman to be jealous of if ever there was one. Yet she held her own, mindful of Geoffrey's hand squeezing hers. "How are you, Danielle?" she asked pleasantly, totally unprepared for the response she was promptly to receive.

"Relieved to see that someone's finally tied this man down. He's haunted the female imagination for far too long. Now that he's out of circulation, we'll all just have to give up our dreams."

"What dreams?" Geoffrey drawled, totally amused. "Your dreams center around one former linebacker—ah, here he comes now." They were joined by a man Sara had never met, whose barrel chest would have been a dead giveaway even without his bull neck.

"Sara, I'd like you to meet Tom Christian. Tom and I play handball together."

"Play?" the larger man echoed on a mocking note, to which Geoffrey rubbed his jaw.

"Come on, Tom. I'm not *that* bad."

"They're impossible," Danielle joked to Sara as she leaned affectionately against Tom's arm. "They have this rivalry going on the court to see who can run who ragged. I'm just waiting for them to collide with each other and knock themselves out cold!"

Sara laughed at the picture as she chased all thought of jealousy from her mind. "That might be worth watching."

"You'll have to come with me sometime," Danielle offered. "I'd love to have someone to talk with. Or we could get our own game going. It gets pretty boring listening to nothing but grunts!"

"All right, ladies," Tom cut in. "If you've had enough amusement at our expense, may I suggest a drink?"

When he disappeared with the orders, another couple approached. Sara recognized the man instantly from the crowd way back then. The woman was, however, quite different from the wife she'd known. As if reading her thoughts, Geoffrey lowered his head to whisper in her ear. "Ted Weston. Phillippa is number two." With a comprehending nod at the Oriental carpeting underfoot, Sara smiled. To the observer, she'd just been whispered sweet nothings by her husband, who then proceeded to nibble the upper curve of her ear and savor the shiver of pleasure that whipped through her before he straightened to greet the new arrivals.

"How are you, Ted?"

"I'm fine," the other exclaimed, accompanying his words with a vigorous handshake. "But I should be asking *you* that question." He shifted his gaze, then hesitated. "Sara . . . ?"

"The same," she said with a smile. "It's nice to see you, Ted."

"Sara," Geoffrey interjected, "this is Phillippa."

Sara nodded. "Phillippa."

"Congratulations to you both," the young woman said softly, more timidly, seeming far less sure of herself than the others. Sara guessed her to be in her mid-twenties, making her significantly younger than her husband. She was also, at close range, suspiciously pregnant.

Once upon a time Sara would have felt instant envy even to the point of depression. Now, though, she had Lizzie. And tonight nothing could dampen her spirits. "And to you," she said with a smile, cocking a brow at the telltale rounding of her middle. "When are you due?"

Phillippa blushed and put a reflexive hand on her stomach. "Not until March, I'm afraid. It seems I've been waiting forever, and I've only now begun to show."

"You look wonderful, Phillippa." Geoffrey added his encouragement. "How are you feeling?"

"Not bad. Tired sometimes."

"The boys keep her running."

Again Geoffrey lowered his voice to explain the situation to Sara, this time, though, in Ted and Phillippa's earshot. "Ted's two boys live with them. They're—how old now, Ted?"

"Thirteen and nine. And noisy?" He rolled his eyes. "Nonstop!"

Sara grinned knowingly. "I came from a family of six, of which four were boys. I can sympathize. And if you're hoping for a nice, quiet, demure little girl this time, don't hold your breath."

Jeff turned to her with a frown. "Don't tell me that *you* were a tomboy."

"Not me—my older sister. She was right in the middle of the guys all the time."

"What's she doing now?" Phillippa asked.

"She's a veterinarian and couldn't be happier."

Ted shook his head. "That's a far cry from your career. Tell us about it."

Sending Geoffrey an apologetic look, Sara shrugged modestly. "What do you want to know?"

And so the evening went. With Geoffrey as impressed as the others, Sara talked shop, politics and the economy right along with the most eloquent and well informed. That she'd been home helping her parents struggle for survival on the farm while they'd been sowing wild oats at exclusive schools and universities was irrelevant. Her cool sophistication was every bit as genuine as theirs.

And she enjoyed herself. Whether or not these people would ever become good friends was a moot point, given the time limitation of her marriage. But she felt at ease with them as she'd never felt before. And she felt simultaneously closer to Geoffrey.

As a couple, they intermeshed perfectly. He seemed to know exactly when she wanted to eat or drink, what she wanted to discuss, with whom she wanted to spend more or less time. Likewise, their interaction couldn't have been better choreographed had they hired a professional in body language to coach them on the signs of love. If Sara was to muse at the skillful show Geoffrey had put on for the sake of the others, he was no less amazed at her own display. It was all so subtle—the hand holding, the shy glances, the exchange of smiles and whispers—subtle and convincing. So convincing that Sara let the aura of it cushion her even through the drive home. It was only in the front hall that reality seeped through.

"That was nice, Jeff," she murmured, slowly drawing off her gloves. "Thank you."

Geoffrey stood behind her, leaning back against the closed front door. "Thank *you*. You handled it very well."

The cool edge to his voice brought her around, evoking the defensiveness that lurked just below the surface. "I wasn't aware of 'handling' anything. As far as I knew, I was being myself."

"I'm sure it had to be something of a strain. You never took to this kind of thing before."

With a sigh Sara let her hands fall to her sides. "Eight years have passed since I last saw those people, Jeff. My life now is very, very different from what it was then. *I'm* very different. To you and your friends, the change may seem momentous. But from my point of view it's been gradual and therefore far less shocking." She'd purposely chosen to touch on the more general social behavior as opposed to the more specific, personal way she'd responded to her husband.

It was a necessary diversion. For looking at him now, she felt the same powerful attraction she had all night. Of all the men at the party—and there had been quite a collection of good-looking ones—none had appealed to her in the least, save Jeff. Even as he stared at her now, his arms crossed over his chest, his eyes dark and strangely enigmatic, she wanted him desperately. In effect, the evening had been one long enticement leading up to a moment that wasn't to be.

If only she were a seductress, she thought then. If only she could approach and bewitch him until the only thought in his mind was of full and wholehearted possession. But she couldn't do that. As self-assured, as sophisticated, as she'd become, as liberated a woman as she was, she simply couldn't do it. There was still that traditional element she needed. He'd rebuffed her in the past when she'd dared to cry out for him. This time he'd have to come to her.

But he didn't. During what seemed hours of silent study of each other, Geoffrey didn't move. His face bore that same mask of control she was quickly coming to despise as a sign of her own failure, her own helplessness. Giving up the fight with a low sigh of defeat, she turned and wordlessly started up the stairs.

Feeling tormented by something that seemed forever out of reach, she showered, drew on her long white gown and, with her blond hair shimmering over her shoulders, padded barefoot along the corridors in the dark of the night to the one place she'd sought solace so long ago. Far to the rear of the first floor of the house, the solarium was a generous circle of a room, one half of which was paneled in glass, one half in white wood, and the entirety of which was landscaped with a lavish assortment of plants. The heavily glassed ceiling that let in sun during the day now gave a copious view of the stars. And even as she blamed her immediate woes on that brilliant full moon above, Sara sank down upon an oversize lounge, stretched out her legs, folded her hands over her stomach and looked up.

The sky was filled with stars. Which was the

first—star light, star bright . . . but what good
were wishes when reality was so hard-boned?
Everything in her marriage was narrowly
aimed toward that year-end point, when Lizzie
would be Geoffrey's and its purpose would be
served. And love? It seemed to be bouncing off
the outer walls of that narrow corridor, never
quite able to penetrate to the core of their marriage. Only when it was shared, she mused,
would it have that power.

Mesmerized by thoughts of stars and love
and eternity, Sara was unaware that Geoffrey
had approached. He stood quietly in the doorway watching her, his tie and jacket gone, his
shirt unbuttoned and hanging loose. He'd
known she would come here as surely as he'd
known of his own need to do so. He'd spent
hours here after she'd left so long ago, then
had discovered her sketches tucked away in
one of the paneled cabinets and had sought
out the room all the more often. Perhaps it was
the openness here, made for hopes and
dreams and the conviction that one day things
would be right. But was it right that she'd conquered *him*, just as she'd conquered every
other man at the party tonight? She was *his*; he
had a right to her!

He took a determined step forward, then

stopped. She was beautiful lying there, an alabaster goddess in the moonlight, serene, ephemeral, tempting beyond imagination. And he thought he could keep his distance—what a pipe dream *that* had been! She had bewitched him . . . and now she dared lie there so peacefully. Revenge; perhaps that had been the underlying motive for her acceptance of his proposal. If so, she was the victor. She'd so commandeered his senses that he hadn't been able to take his eyes from her tonight. Damn it, he wanted her as he'd never wanted anyone else! Then he clenched his jaw. If it was revenge she savored, she'd had her moment. Now his was fast approaching.

At the sound of his slow steps, Sara was shaken from her trance. Looking quickly in the direction of the quiet tap, she held her breath. When Geoffrey emerged from shadow to moonlight, her heart began to thud. She couldn't move, couldn't speak, simply watched him approach until his moon shadow fell on her.

Had it not been for the halo effect around his head, she might have thought him the devil. He'd invaded her peace of mind for days—no, years. And now he stood over her, tall and straight, and in full cognizance of his power.

His movements controlled, he slowly sat down by her hip. With his face that much closer, she could follow the direction of his sight. When he studied her features intently, she returned a wide-eyed gaze. Then his eyes dropped to her throat and she swallowed hard; then as he looked at her breasts, she grew all the more aware of the thunderous hammer of her heart. Little was hidden from him beneath the thin satin of her gown, and he took in sensuous details that altered even as he watched.

Sara was as vulnerable as she'd ever been. She wanted him badly, yet she couldn't reach for him. His silence frightened her, yet she couldn't speak out against it. That he desired her was no mystery; it was his motive she couldn't fathom. All she could do was lie still beneath his gaze, indulging her body its growing arousal, in fact, helpless to stem it.

Contrarily, Geoffrey's hands were steady when he reached to slide his thumbs beneath the thin straps of her gown. When he eased them slowly over the curves of her shoulders and down her arms, Sara bit her lip. Would he lead her on again, only to call a halt at the moment of humiliation when her desire was such that she begged for him? She started to shake her head slowly, but he held her chin steady, then let his hand shimmer back down her body to that strap he'd momentarily abandoned. Inch by inch her breasts were bared as he eased the gown lower.

She'd begun to breathe more heavily now. "Jeff," she whispered, "don't . . . do this to me . . ."

His voice was a deep rumble of male need. "You're mine, Sara. For the year, you're mine." He worked the gown to her waist, then drew the straps over her hands and slid the fabric lower. "So help me, I've tried to stay away. But I can't bear looking at you, wanting you all the time. I may be damned for it, but while you're here I intend to take my fill."

She should have been livid at his callously male expression, yet all she felt was a surge of relief. She needed him as badly as he needed her. And yes, she might well be damned for it, but—but—she wanted *her* fill as well.

"This time there'll be no rushing," he went on, his voice growing thicker when the gown reached her thighs. He paused for a minute to savor what he'd uncovered. For the first time, then, he seemed affected, his hands slightly less steady when he pushed the fabric free of her feet and let it fall to the floor.

Lying naked before him, Sara felt paralyzed.

His eyes slid up her body, halting here and there, searing her at every stop. She felt a trembling deep inside and knew he had to be aware of it, yet he made no move to hold her—not yet. Rather, he sat straighter and shrugged out of his shirt, dropping it carelessly, his eyes ever on her body.

The play of the moonlight enhanced the muscularity of his shoulders, broad sinewed but smooth, and his tapering torso. Had she been able, she would have reached to admire the maturity the years had brought to him. But just then he took her wrists and pinned them to the lounge on either side of her shoulders. Then slowly, slowly he lowered his head. His lips were gentle in a forceful kind of way, brooking no argument when they opened her mouth, allowing her no recourse but to submit to his liking. Not that she would have objected; she was easily swept along in the torrent of desire that stirred from within and molded her as surely as that firm man above.

It was the flow of heat through her veins that warmed her body, for Geoffrey steadfastly held himself away. He only touched her wrists and her lips. All the rest was left to ache for him.

She moaned softly when he shifted to press moist kisses along the line of her jaw, and closed her eyes when the hot torment moved on to cascade down her throat. Still her wrists were pinioned, frustrating her need to touch him. Her fingernails dug sharply into her palm when his lips opened over her breast to allow him a taste of her ripeness. With the moist and alluring friction of his tongue, he explored the full swell of her flesh. Needing more, she gasped for air and arched upward until, at last, he took her nipple into his mouth and sucked on it deeply.

Sara felt the pull to her core, that core which was all woman, all his. It seemed only natural when he moved lower, sampling each sweet curve and indentation along an inevitable path. When her hands were suddenly freed, she could only thrust them into the lush vibrancy of his hair to hold him closer, knowing as she did that this was the only reality that mattered. Despite his talk of rights and possession, he worshiped her as no other man had done before or after. Her body was his, aflame with desire, and her only misgiving was that she seemed helpless to express her love.

Then his fingers spanned her thighs, spreading them, and his lips moved downward, downward toward her warmth. "Jeff . . . don't . . ."

He barely raised his head. "But I want to, Sara."

"Please . . ." she whispered, but he didn't answer. When his tongue moved against her she gave a helpless cry and arched away. But he was determined, persisting in his quest until modesty vanished and she writhed in pleasure. Her breathing came faster, her hands clutched his hair. She knew the beauty of mindless surrender to the power of the white-hot pulse that raged through her. Then she cried his name once and caught her breath as a wave of sensation erupted deep within. When she could think once again, Geoffrey was beside her, his hands moving tenderly over her body.

"I . . . I didn't want . . . that . . ." she gasped.

"I did," he countered, but his voice was gentle. "I've dreamed of it for years."

"But what about you? What about *your* satisfaction?"

"That *was* part of my satisfaction. And we have the whole night."

It would have been the perfect time for him to sweep her up into his arms and carry her off to his bedroom. Having played the loving couple all evening, what would have been more fitting? But Geoffrey had other things in mind as he nibbled her lips tauntingly. His fingers found tender spots and caressed them as he whispered soft words of desire. Far sooner than Sara would have imagined possible, satiation faded, and her body came alive to his once more.

With a soft moan she yielded to his lure, simultaneously wanting nothing more than to bring him to a mindless height of arousal. And having been relieved of her own urgency, she was in an ideal position to do just that. Little did it matter, she told herself, that they weren't in the master bedroom. After all, what could be more romantic than the stars overhead and that bright full moon?

Lifting her hands to his shoulders, Sara released all inhibition and began a tactile exploration that had Geoffrey breathing heavily within minutes. Kneading his flesh, her fingers moved down his arms and then to his chest, where she ran her palms across the firmly muscled expanse, pausing only to tease twin male nipples before sliding her hands to his back and drawing him closer.

When she arched her back, her breasts touched him. With a ragged moan, he completed the circle, securing his arms around her and crushing her up against him. "I need you,

Sara," he whispered in a tone that suggested he hadn't meant to speak. But she heard him and she knew that what he'd said made it all worthwhile. He needed her, perhaps at this moment only physically, but he needed her nonetheless. Just as he'd needed her at the funeral. Just as he'd needed her that night to help him forget. Just as, in many ways, he needed her to help resolve his dilemma with Lizzie. And Sara needed to be needed. It was the one element no business victory could provide in her life.

Opening her lips to his, she gave of herself freely, meeting his growing ardor with her own, yet ever conscious of her lover's pleasure. When Geoffrey twisted and came down on his back, she arched gracefully over him, enjoying the freedom the position offered, taking advantage of the leverage. She traced the line of his jaw with her lips, then kissed his neck while she savored the strength of his hands on her back and the bare length of her side. Only when his hands touched her hips did she realize what she was missing.

With a final warm kiss to his lips, she knelt by his side and went to work on the buckle of his belt. When her fingers trembled, she persisted, drawing strength from his reassuring gaze. The belt hung loose and she struggled with the zipper, finally needing help for a problem that wasn't solely hers. But given his rising ardency, Geoffrey struggled likewise. His own hands weren't that much steadier than hers, and his breathing was much less quiet. Finally he swung his legs off the far side of the lounge, kicked off his shoes and socks, stood and hurriedly discarded his pants. But before he could touch his briefs, Sara was on her feet before him, her hands on his wrists, raising them to her shoulders. Looking up at him, she moved his hands slowly downward until they covered her breasts. Only then did she release them to snake her arms up around his neck. Standing on tiptoe then, she kissed him deeply, using her tongue as the counterpoint to his teasing fingers.

How long they stood there, she didn't know, so swept up was she in his passion. They felt and caressed each other's body, finding satisfaction in resultant moans and whispers. When Sara could stand no more of the suspense, she lowered her hands and slipped them beneath the elastic of his briefs, finding him, holding him, wanting nothing more than to surround him with her warmth.

As though needing that too, Geoffrey

tugged off the briefs, all the while kissing her hungrily. Then, bringing her down on top of him, he fell back onto the lounge where it all began again, the touching and exploring and fondling. When Sara feared her patience was nearly exhausted, she moved over him, straddling his hips, teasing him for that last urgent moment before he took her, lifted her, brought her slowly, sensuously down.

If Sara thought she'd been in control, she was joyously mistaken. Impassioned as Geoffrey was, he set the rhythm, guiding her forward, then back as the pace demanded. Her back was bowed gracefully over his body to allow her lips access to his. Her breasts rubbed electrically against his chest. And the heat between them rose slowly, then with growing speed until there was nothing but her and him and their fierce need for one another. It was a fiery moment, that last, one that raged, then exploded and seemed to envelop them in its brilliance before slowly, slowly cooling and leaving them drained.

Sara collapsed on top of Geoffrey, her breathing as jagged as his. But he held her there, mindless of her meager weight, reluctant to let the moment end.

"We have the whole night," he'd said earlier, and as the haze of passion slowly lifted from Sara's benumbed mind she recalled his words and wondered what would happen— now . . . tomorrow . . . next month. She knew she was in trouble. For with each passing day she seemed to love him all the more. With each passing night she needed him all the more. What did the future hold, she asked herself in trepidation?

Eight

The moonlight played games, momentarily giving Geoffrey's face a look of love such that Sara's hopes soared. Nor was she discouraged when he eased her to his side, slid off the lounge and lifted her into his arms. It was as she'd imagined before, being carried off in the dark toward a night of passion in his bed.

But it wasn't his bed to which she was carried. And when she felt the chill of her own sheets against her back, the sinking feeling in her stomach was overpowering. Much as she might have hoped to have been his wife, she was still a guest in Geoffrey's house. His returning her here was proof.

Hurt, she opened her mouth to protest when he came down half over her, but her words drowned in a kiss so potent as to stem rebellion at its birth. When he began to caress her again, she forgot everything but his touch, surrendering to the force of her love for him. For though the dark added a kind of anonymity to their passion, it also allowed for free rein of the imagination—in Sara's case, that Geoffrey returned her love.

All night she gloried in the fantasy, finding ecstasy in his arms again and again. No words were spoken save those of passion, and these were shared as in a dream. When she awoke in the morning, however, the dream was over and she was alone. Laid neatly across the foot of the bed was the nightgown that had been discarded in the solarium; Geoffrey must have risen and retrieved their clothes before dawn.

Mercifully she'd slept, or she might have begged him to stay, to preserve the illusion a little longer. But his message was clear. The use of separate bedrooms in opposite wings of the house was symbolic of the distance he wanted to maintain. As he'd implied so vehemently when he'd first come to her last night, she was his for the year, to be used at his will.

As for his bedroom, it was his own inner sanctum, one she wasn't to disturb.

Feeling angry at Geoffrey for his attitude and angry at herself for loving him so much that she was willing to bear it temporarily, she showered, dressed and headed for the kitchen and a cup of tea. To her initial chagrin, Geoffrey was there. To her subsequent amazement, he greeted her as though he were oblivious to any problem whatsoever, which infuriated her all the more.

He was seated at the island counter with a cup of coffee and the newspaper. When she appeared in the doorway, he looked quickly up, smiled and put the paper down. "Hi, Sara. I was wondering when you'd get up. Can I fix you some breakfast?"

It was sheer momentum that brought her nearly to the middle of the room. "Where's Mrs. Fleming?" she asked, trying desperately to ignore that dimple in his cheek.

"She's gone upstairs to clean." He smiled slightly, making the dimple all the more roguish. "We're both—a little late."

It took Sara's utmost control to maintain an even tone. "Is Lizzie up?"

"Are you kidding? She's been at it since seven. You mean you didn't hear her?"

"I'm at the furthest end of the house."

For the first time he acknowledged the edge to her voice. "Does that bother you?"

"Of course not!" Like hell.

"You could move closer if you wanted."

At what price, she wondered? "My room is fine."

He paused then, eyeing her enigmatically. "So, what'll it be? An omelet? French toast? Eggs benedict?"

"You really know how to make all those?"

"I can try," he answered, sobering to add, "which is more than you're doing right now."

Sara was instantly defensive. "And what is *that* supposed to mean?"

She saw him sit straighter, saw the muscle of his jaw begin to work. "It means that you could try to be pleasant. God only knows I am."

It was one straw too many. With a long, pointed glance she whirled and headed angrily toward the door. "If it's that much of an effort, please relax," she called over her shoulder. "I think I can use fresh air better than breakfast."

Geoffrey was beside her instantly, grabbing her arm to halt her escape. "What's wrong, Sara?"

She looked away from him. "Nothing."

"Sara . . ." His voice held a warning which she proceeded to ignore.

"Let go of my arm, Jeff."

"Not until you tell me what's bothering you."

Her head swiveled, and her gaze shot up at him. "You really don't know?"

"No. I really don't know. After last night—"

"Please, Jeff! Don't bring that up."

"Then tell me what's the matter."

With a deep sigh she turned her head away. "If you don't already know, I'm afraid I can't help you."

Perplexed, Geoffrey opened his mouth to argue, only to shut it moments later and release her arm. As he watched her disappear down the hall toward the front door, he was more confused than ever. He was sure she'd been pleased last night. Hell, if he hadn't known better, he might have imagined her as much in love as he was. She'd responded with such abandon. He could never get enough of her. But, then, he should know better. She'd made a deal. She'd agreed to be his wife in return for his helping her set up her branch office. Even now he knew he'd find her in the cottage.

Without quite having made a conscious decision, he quickly found himself there, too. She was standing amid a mess of boards and saw-dust and didn't look up when he entered.

"Let's have this out, Sara."

"There's nothing to say, Geoffrey. Leave well enough alone."

"It's not well enough!" he yelled loudly enough to corral her immediate attention. When he came to stand before her, she willed her legs to steadiness. "I want to know what's behind these sudden turnarounds every time we make love. You enjoy yourself—and don't try to tell me you don't. But then you turn your back on me, or wake up on the wrong side of the bed."

Her eyes flashed. "If it's the wrong side of the bed I've woken up on, it's only because you were occupying the right side for most of the night. If you'd stayed away from me in the first place, I would have been just where I wanted to be."

"And where's that? Alone? Frustrated? Is that what you want in life?" His nostrils flared under the pressure of self-restraint. "Or is it just that your precious business gives you more satisfaction than any man could?" He lowered his voice to a dangerous growl. "Is that it, Sara? Does it turn you on, the power

you feel? Have you sacrificed humanity for a—
a *thing*?"

"No!" she whispered, her heart pounding in
her chest. "That's not it at all!"

"Then what is? What is it that makes you
tick?"

Her hesitation was brief, her voice speaking
a heartfelt vow. "Survival, Geoffrey! I was
weaned on it, grew up on it, was introduced to
adulthood with it in tow. Why do you think I
left you eight years ago?" Against her will, her
eyes flooded. "In the end it still seemed best to
salvage what little was left of my dream and
seek its fulfillment elsewhere. I've tried. God
only knows, I've tried." Overcome with emotion, she lowered her head and squeezed her
eyes shut. "Yes, I want you at night," she whispered brokenly. "I won't deny it. But I can't
help, when it's over, there is always this anger
and the memories of that old hurt." Her fists
clenched by her sides, she felt herself waver.
Within instants Geoffrey drew her against him,
offering the quiet, undemanding support she
needed.

"Shhhh, princess." He spoke softly against
her hair, torn once more by guilt about all that
had happened so long ago. "It's all right. Look,
I'm sorry I pushed you. I know that you're

under a lot of pressure. It's just that . . ." He
took a deep breath. "It's just that I don't want
to fight with you. And I don't want to see you
miserable every time we're together." His
arms gently circled her back, barely moving.
"What I want is for you to be able to enjoy
what we have without self-recrimination."

She drew her head back to look at him. "You
want me to take it all lightly, with a grain of
salt?" she asked, feeling hurt all over again.

Looking down at her, Geoffrey sighed. "No,
Sara. That's not what I want at all. I want you
to let things happen. Just to . . . let things take
their own course."

That was precisely the problem, she mused.
The course was a dead-end one with a year's
limit. "I'm not very good at that type of thing.
For the past eight years I've been in control of
everything I've done. I don't know if—"

"Try, Sara. If not for yourself or me, then
for . . . for . . ." He paused, reluctant but desperate. "For Lizzie. If there's tension between
us, she'll pick it up in a minute. Don't you think
she's been through enough?" He knew he was
unfairly playing on her sentiments, but he had
no other recourse. When Sara shot him a cutting glance, he felt all the more guilty. But if

the tactic would buy him her good humor, it would be worth the underhandedness.

"That's cheating," she accused him, but her voice had lost its edge. "There was nothing in our deal that ruled out tension."

"Do *you* want it?"

Her tone softened. "No."

"Then what are we arguing about?"

For a split second she wasn't sure. She'd been hurt and angry before. Now, with Geoffrey's lean frame supporting her, with his arms cradling her and his broad shoulders sheltering her, she felt totally pacified. Granted, she wished that tender look on his face was for her as well as for Lizzie, but then the child needed it all the more. At least Sara still had the business and her life in New York.

As though riding her brain wave back to the scene, Geoffrey looked around. "Pretty messy, isn't it?"

Standing back as his arms dropped, she followed his gaze in a sweeping arc. "It'll be great, though, when they're done. Especially the workshop. Have you seen it?"

"Not since Friday morning."

On impulse she put out her hand. With a concrete source of excitement to share, she was quick to shift her frustration to the back burner. And she really didn't want to fight, either. "Come on. Let me show you." She led him up the narrow stairs to what had once been the attic. "They cut the skylights on Friday afternoon. It'll be fantastic to work up here." Side by side they stood looking first at the ceiling, then at the rest of the single room with its embryonic booths and benches.

"Are you pleased with what they're doing?"

"Oh, yes! They've managed to follow my scribbles exactly!" She wandered to examine the beginnings of a workbench, then turned to face Geoffrey. "I can't wait to work up here. It's so bright and cheery. I only hope I have the time." Her thoughts were of the family she'd temporarily acquired and the growing desire she had to be with them.

"*Make* the time."

She chuckled. "Easier said than done. You of all people should know that. When was the last time you worked on the original design for one of your buildings?"

He arched a brow. "Hmmmm . . ."

"You know, you really should do some of that, Geoffrey. You're very talented."

His gaze shifted to the window. "Your opinion is based on a few drawings done over fifteen years ago. That training was as much of an indulgence as my mother would allow. I'm sure I've lost most of what I had. And besides, you're right. I barely have time to screen the architects we hire, let alone do their work for them!"

She rested gingerly against the protruding pine shelf, crossed her arms over her breasts and eyed him speculatively. "I bet you could have done a better job than me designing this office."

"No way! I know nothing about jewelry making. As a matter of fact, you've been very stingy with that information. Come on. Tell me. How do you do it?"

Sara stifled a smile as she pondered his half-comical expression. Then she shrugged, feeling suddenly more confident. That Geoffrey respected her knowledge of the craft was encouraging. "Oh"—she wrinkled her nose—"it's really simple. You take a piece of gold and work over it for a while, hammering and annealing and pickling and cleaning—"

"Pickling?"

"Sure. You see, when you heat a piece of metal in the process of working on it, the surface becomes dirty—oxidized. To clean it, you drop it in a solution of water and sulfuric acid—a pickle solution."

"Must smell great."

She cocked her head toward the ceiling vents strategically placed beneath eaves to be effective yet practically unseen. "It would be pretty bad without those. But it's a necessary stage."

"Where did you learn all this?"

Again she shrugged, this time growing more pensive. "Oh, I picked it up here and there."

"Here and there? This wasn't all in Tucson?"

"Actually, no. I spent time in Dallas and Fort Worth and St. Paul—even in Providence, Rhode Island. After I'd mastered the art of making earrings out of beads and wire in Tucson, I apprenticed myself to a silversmith in Dallas and worked for him in exchange for lessons. As I wanted to learn another process, I moved on. The whole thing snowballed, so to speak. Each place I went to, I learned more, made more contacts. I sold jewelry all along the way. By the time I reached New York I was actually able to afford a small studio. From there"—she gestured with her hand—"well, things just took off."

"I'll say," Geoffrey murmured, shaking his head in slow amazement. "And it's going to be worse when you open for business here. Have you any idea how many inquiries I've received already?"

Sara's eyes widened. "Really? What did you tell them?"

"I told them it would be at least a month before you'd be able to meet with anyone. That is how you work it, isn't it?"

"Uh-huh. Before I put anything on paper, I like to talk with the client. Since each piece is custom designed, it's critical to know the personality of the wearer, the purpose for which the piece is to be worn." Her eyes glowed. "That's where so much of the challenge comes in. I love it."

"It's obvious," he said softly, wondering once again whether she had room for any other love in her life. But as jealous as he was of this abundant enthusiasm for her work, he did enjoy seeing it. When she lit up that way, she was positively gorgeous. Perhaps one day . . . but no, it wouldn't do to get his hopes up. He cleared his throat. "Do you prefer working in gold?"

"Personally, yes." She glanced down at her wedding band, so wide yet simple and brightly reflecting the skylights. "It's a—a happy metal. There are others that are as beautiful but that strike me differently. That's why I need to hear a client's preference. If it were up to me, I'd do *everything* in gold." For a minute she feared she'd said too much. Feeling shy, she kept her eyes averted, daring to look at him only when he spoke again. To her relief, if he'd suspected the strength of her feelings regarding not only that gold band on her finger but the one on his, he diplomatically avoided mention of it. Rather, he settled back against a windowsill.

"You work with stones too, though. Do you have preferences there?"

"Again, it depends on the client and the occasion and the particular outfit, if there is one, that the piece is to match. The bracelet and earrings that I wore last night are perfect examples. The ivory was necessary to carry on the white motif—though it took me a while to find a piece of ivory that was just the right shade. I've done quite a few things in pearl or smoky topaz, or black onyx, amethyst or jade."

"But your favorite," he persisted. "Personally. If you were to turn the tables and have a dress designed to match a piece of jewelry, so that you could design the bracelet or necklace or earring of any stone you wanted, what would you choose?"

Looking down, she thought for a minute. The answer was simple. Of the four most precious gems, there was one she'd never worked with. It carried too much of an emotional connotation for her. One day . . . maybe one day she'd be able to do it. Until then it would simply remain a dream.

"I adore working with gemstones." She smiled on a note of quiet awe that was not wholly untruthful. "Rubies, sapphires, emeralds," she softly named the other three. "They're the most brilliant, the most colorful, the most precious. Each one is unique."

So very much was left unsaid, yet as they stood in silent regard of one another, Sara had to wonder if Geoffrey understood. Once more she felt herself being drawn into the depth of his gaze, and she welcomed its warmth. But when the sun passed behind a cloud and the light above dimmed in poignant reminder of the fleeting nature of their relationship, she shivered.

"Cold?" he asked, coming quickly to her side.

She grimaced toward the ceiling, ad-libbing

perfectly. "It'll help when they get the glass up there tomorrow."

"Come." He threw a gentle arm around her shoulder. "Let's go back to the house. You haven't even got a sweater on."

It was true. When she'd stamped out so angrily, she'd been oblivious to the fact that the tunic top over her jeans was, albeit long sleeved, a single cotton layer. With the chill in the air and the open-air state of the roof, she could have used a sweater or a shawl—not that she had any objection to the warmth of Geoffrey's arm as it tucked her against him.

Side by side they started down the stairs, jostling one another, laughing, finally separating and going down single file. At the bottom he turned with his hands on his hips and cast a calculating eye back at the narrow stairway. "This has to be widened. That's all there is to it."

"Don't be silly, Jeff. I'll probably be the only one to use it."

He frowned momentarily. "You mean you won't have a team doing the actual work out here?"

It was something she'd carefully thought out, a decision she'd reached only after hours of discussion with her people in New York.

"Not at first." Which meant, practically speaking, given the time limit of their relationship, probably never. "I'm going to try to do special pieces here, but most of the rest will continue to be done in New York. If I feel that the demand merits it, I may hire someone. But aside from the work I do myself, this office will be more for the contracting and designing end of it."

After pondering her words, Geoffrey nodded. "Then it should be widened for safety's sake."

"But, Jeff—"

He held up a large hand. "No more arguments. Understood?"

What she understood was the deeper meaning of his quiet plea. For a minute she simply stared up at him. Then she spoke softly. "I'll try, Jeff. I can't make any promises. But I will try."

They'd come full circle in the morning's discussion. Geoffrey returned her gaze for infinite seconds longer. "Fair enough," he said, then slowly extended a hand to her. She took it readily and allowed herself to be drawn to his side as they walked back toward the house. His motive was peace. She knew that. She also knew that it was the most practical motive he might have. A year—slightly less now—could be a long, long time if they were forever at each other's throats. And then, as he'd so carefully pointed out, there was Lizzie, who did deserve whatever happiness they could give her. He might be playing a mean game, but he was right. And she *would* try, she vowed, taking strength from the fingers that were covering hers.

"And you can really make an omelet?" she teased, looking up through the shade of her lashes and feeling better than she had since she'd awoken.

He smiled crookedly. "It might not look all that pretty but it sure tastes fantastic."

In the end anything would probably have tasted fantastic, given Sara's improved mood. Sure enough, Geoffrey did make an omelet, filled—actually, brimming, as he'd warned— with ham and cheese and onion and green pepper. To watch him slice up the works was a treat, as was the easy conversation that ran gently throughout. He spoke of his work, of the new condominium complex being built downtown, of the paper plant in Oregon that had just been renovated, of the electronics division's recent entry into the world of robotics. Later, after they'd somewhat guiltily left the dishes for Mrs. Fleming, they went in search of

Lizzie, over whose head they resumed their discussion of Sara's work. She took pride in relating anecdotes of her experiences with various illustrious clients, sharing tales of last-minute hair-raisers and close calls that were humorous only in hindsight.

Despite its inauspicious beginnings, it was a day whose pleasure was shadowed only by Sara's knowledge that she'd be on a plane by noon Monday, headed back to New York for the week. Had it been the long holiday weekend, she asked herself as she reflected on how much she wished she could stay? Had she simply settled in so much that the unsettling was much harder than it had been before?

If only that were the case, she mused the next day as her jumbo jet rose high above San Francisco, headed east. If only it were as simple as that. No, it was Jeff she'd be missing during those next four days. Jeff and, yes, Lizzie. As a threesome, they meshed perfectly, the fulfillment of one part of Sara's dream. She couldn't recall another Thanksgiving weekend when she'd been happier. But now she was returning to New York alone.

In a moment's daydream she wondered at the fun she'd have showing Jeff the Big Apple.

Oh, yes, he'd been there many times, but never to see *her* friends, *her* work, *her* world. He'd snow them all, she knew it. Perhaps one day she could convince him to come.

But, then, his world was the child. Would he leave her alone long enough to make the trip? As a matter of fact, he could bring her, Sara realized, smiling at the thought of their pushing her stroller through Central Park on a sunny afternoon. Initial doubts notwithstanding, she'd found mothering Lizzie to be one of the most natural things she'd ever done, and rewarding now that the little one's arms wound readily around her neck, her ruddy cheek nestled easily against her shoulder and her eyes lit in recognition when she entered the room. As Sara had feared, she was quickly coming to love the child. A dangerous thing—very dangerous— for them both. And Jeff? What about him? Though she loved him to distraction, he remained an enigma. For every bout of passion or even simple companionship they shared, there remained a barrier between them. Much as she might have wished it, he never once made mention of love. What about him?

Geoffrey watched the next few weeks pass, growing more and more perplexed. Where he'd expected—half hoped for the sake of his heart—to find a hardened businesswoman, he found a woman of warmth and compassion. Where he'd expected to find a woman skilled solely in her narrow field, he found a woman who seemed remarkably able to tackle almost anything. And where he'd expected to find a woman who abided the presence of a child purely for the sake of the bargain, he found a woman who rose naturally and enthusiastically to the challenge of motherhood.

There was Lizzie's room, now completed and adorable, from the gay ruffled curtains that matched the wallpaper to the bright green carpeting on the floor and the musical lamp on the dresser and the polka-dot bumpers on the crib. There were small gifts and huge hugs with each return trip from New York, and a birthday party replete with balloons and cake and a stuffed but life-size St. Bernard dog to stand guard in a corner of her room. And there was a genuine affection between Sara and Lizzie that stirred him deeply. At times he'd sit back and watch them together, one head as blond as the next, one smile as sweet as the other, and he'd find it hard to believe that Lizzie wasn't Sara's own. Then he'd stop and remind himself that it wasn't to be, and his thoughts would darken.

For with each passing day, with each passing week, he grew more convinced of his need for Sara. He'd never experienced such emotional fulfillment as during the time he spent with her. Certainly Lizzie's presence filled a need he'd had, but this was different. Much as a man might try to devote himself solely to the well-being of a child, it was a woman he needed.

But Sara was only half his, and that half was his for too short a time. Would he ever understand her—seeming so happy at times with him yet regularly stepping back on that plane bound for New York? And once she was there, did she resent the time she spent with him? Or did she value it for the sake of her business?

And then there were the nights, after they'd offered polite words to one another and gone their own ways. In moments of equivocation he'd debated the merits of the act, yet found himself nonetheless on his way to the guest wing. At night; always at night. And always in her room. What a futile gesture that was, his feeble attempt to convince himself that she couldn't take her place in his bed, hence in his heart. But damn it, she was there! And then when she responded with such willingness, such eagerness—as close to loving as any man might wish—but in the dark, with only sighs and moans of pleasure and never a word of love. Was she dreaming of others at those times? No, she cried his name as often as he did hers. Then what did go through her mind when she was in his arms? What did *she* think of the future?

Though he hadn't intended it at first, he saw himself increasingly involving her in his life. He'd promised that Lizzie would be cared for by a nurse, yet they spent as much time with the child each day as many another set of parents. And there had been other evening engagements after that first—a party at the club, an evening at the theater, dinner at some of the finest restaurants San Francisco had to offer. And she took to it without argument. Was she simply doing it for the child's sake, as he'd asked? But she seemed so happy.

He thought back to the eighteen-year-old he'd married ten years before. Then he'd seen in Sara the promise of warmth, home and family. Now, whatever her reasons, she was all that. He couldn't have asked for more—other than that it be for real. He'd given her the out he now dreaded—that time span the end of which hung heavy on his own happiness. And for the life of him he didn't know what to do.

Christmas came and went, a beautifully peaceful day, the nicest part of which, from Sara's point of view, was the prospect of spending the week to come with Geoffrey and Lizzie. Everything was taken care of in New York. The cottage was furnished and operational. For the first time she was able to shift from home to work without having to board an airplane.

And it was a luxury she fully appreciated, for the commute had begun to take its toll. She was tired. Those idle air hours during which she had nothing to do but brood about when it would all be over did little for her peace of mind. When she was with Jeff or Lizzie she was the happiest, determinedly avoiding all thoughts of the future. During the week preceding New Year's, such times were in abundance.

It was at one such time, an evening when Lizzie was asleep and they sat beside one another on the sofa in the den before the fire, that Geoffrey turned to Sara, his eyes thoughtful. "Will you mind spending New Year's Eve alone, just the two of us?" he asked quietly.

"Of course not. Did you think I would?"

"I didn't know. You've become a very social being of late."

"Not really of late, Jeff," she chided softly, gently. "You just haven't been around during the past few years."

"But you do seem to enjoy yourself when we go out."

"Why shouldn't I? Your friends are nice."

He arched a brow in skepticism. "I can remember a time when you couldn't stand them."

"I was very young then, without a drop of confidence. I had nothing going for me—"

"That wasn't true."

"I *felt* that I had nothing going for me," she softly corrected herself. "That *was* true. I felt awkward and out of it." She paused, thinking how comfortable she felt at the moment, sitting, talking quietly with her husband. "Things are different now. What I am—what my business is—I don't feel intimidated anymore."

He took her hand and studied its slender lines. "That much is obvious, whether or not it was justified in the first place. But"—he looked up—"would you feel comfortable entertaining them here?" He'd toyed with the idea for days and only now, with the atmosphere of warmth between them, had he felt the courage to broach it.

"Sure," she answered without batting an eyelash. She knew what he didn't—that she'd entertained any number of times in New York—and the thought gave her all the more confidence.

"Sure?" His smile was lopsided. "Just like that?"

"Why not? What did you have in mind?"

"A dinner party."

She beamed. "My specialty."

"You're being facetious."

"No, I'm serious. Tell me what you want. A dinner party for how many?"

He held her gaze, testing her. "Thirty?"

"Thirty! Whew, that's some dinner party."

"Too much?"

"No, no. It's no problem from my angle." She frowned, growing pensive. "I suppose we could rent tables and put a few in each of several different rooms."

"We could?"

She had to laugh at the surprise in his voice. "Sure. How else could we handle that many?"

"We could have a buffet."

She crinkled her nose. "A buffet often seems

so rushed. If we're going to do it, we might as well do it right. Any special reason for the event, or is it just your turn?"

"You make it sound heartless."

"If the only reason you're doing it is to reciprocate for invitations you've received, I suppose it is heartless."

Undaunted, he squeezed her hand. "In this case I can assure you it's not. Yes, there may be some people I'd like to invite who've entertained me within the past few months. And there are certainly those with whom we've spent time recently. But there are others I'd like you to meet, including some media people who might just be able to give you a little publicity now that your office is finally open."

"So this is a debut?" She drawled the word with fitting tongue-in-cheek humor.

He grinned. "If you will."

"And you want it to be held—yesterday?" Still that humor. She was actually excited at the prospect of showing him what she could do as a hostess now, ten years later.

"Mid-January will be fine," he assured her, his outer amusement masking that inner wonder. Would she really do it? Could she?

"Great! I'll get to work on it tomorrow. But

tell me, have we got any champagne in the cellar?"

"For the party?"

"For New Year's Eve. If we're set on doing things right . . ."

New Year's Eve was as right as it could be. It was quiet, intimate and warm. Sara felt her love for Geoffrey flow as freely as the champagne he uncorked. Her only sadness occurred when she thought of the next year's celebration—sadness and confusion. It simply didn't make sense that two people who seemed to get along as well as they did couldn't make a go of their marriage on a permanent basis. Did Geoffrey love her? He seemed to; yet he never said it. What were his thoughts? Was he still only looking for a partner in the adoption, or had she managed to get under his skin even a little? She was a modern woman; she should ask. But she couldn't, for fear she'd hear the worst. *Coward*, she called herself more than once. But she didn't say a word lest she rock the boat on which they'd finally found such an even keel. Besides, she was so happy this way—ignorance *was* bliss. If she could only keep from wondering . . .

As it happened, the New Year took off at such a breathless clip that she had little time to think.

Nine

No sooner had Sara returned to New York than Geoffrey got word of the preliminary processing of the adoption papers and an interview scheduled for that Friday morning. Quickly shifting appointments, Sara zipped back to the West Coast two short days after she'd left. That the meeting with the court social worker went well was justification for the rush. That Geoffrey seemed particularly pleased was compensation for her fatigue. That she was back in San Francisco, with him, with Lizzie, even after so brief an absence, made it all the more worthwhile.

There was, though, no rest for the weary.

The phone in the cottage office didn't stop ringing on Saturday. Sara used Sunday to make preliminary plans for the party. On Monday it was business as usual, on the phone again, primarily long distance to New York. In truth, she found it surprisingly easy to carry on work this way, even with the crunch on for the benefit to be held, coincidentally, a week after the party. Her New York staff had risen to the occasion, handling everything they could, saving those other things for the two or three days of the week that she'd be there with them.

Though things went smoothly into that second week in January, there were random moments of exhaustion when Sara wondered whether she had indeed tackled too much. For in addition to business matters and party plans, there were still Jeff and Lizzie, each of whom took large chunks of her time. They didn't demand it; she gave it freely. And she wouldn't have had it any other way. She *wanted* to spend time with Jeff each morning at breakfast, then later each evening, talking quietly of the day's events. She *wanted* to care for Lizzie, feeding her and bathing her whenever possible, reading to her and playing with her, even taking her for her checkup to finally meet the pediatrician about whom Jeff had raved. And if spending this time with her family—as she very definitely had come to think of Jeff and Lizzie—meant working all the harder at odd points during the day, she felt the trade-off was justified.

Then, two days before the dinner party, a call came in at eight in the morning while Sara and Jeff were having breakfast.

"Trouble?" Geoffrey asked, growing alert when Sara returned from the library white-faced.

"It was the office. David's sick." David was her executive vice president, whose watchful eye had replaced her own and guided things in New York during her absences. Distracted, she slid down against the windowsill and stared blindly at the floor.

"What's wrong?"

"They aren't sure. He woke up in the middle of the night with chest pains. His wife is with him in the hospital." She shook her head slowly, then looked up. "I've got to go back."

"Fly to New York, today? You can't do that, Sara. You just flew out yesterday!"

For an instant her gaze hardened. "Can't? Our bargain doesn't allow for emergencies?"

Geoffrey turned to face her more fully, his tone every bit as deep and hard as her gaze.

"That's not what I meant and you know it! If you insist on whipping back to New York, be my guest. I was thinking of you and that list you rattled off last night of things that you had to do today and tomorrow."

Realizing her error, she looked away. Had she actually grown more defensive, or was she simply tired, and therefore more sensitive? It was obvious from his instant response that he did intend the best.

She spoke more softly. "Those things will just have to wait. First I'd like to see how David is. He's been with me since I opened shop in New York and is a special person. Besides"— she frowned—"with that benefit coming up in little over a week, someone has to keep on top of things. If I fly there today, I'll have all of tomorrow to touch bases. Then I can fly back on Saturday morning and be here in plenty of time for the party."

Pushing his chair from the table, Geoffrey stood. "But you're exhausted already! Take a look at yourself. All week you've been pale. This schedule you've set for yourself isn't healthy." And since her schedule and its grueling nature was largely his fault, he felt guilty.

"It'll work out, Jeff. Really it will. Things are pretty much set for the party. The caterers know what to do; same with the florist. I can make a list of the other things and Mrs. Fleming can follow up on them. While I'm in New York I'll take care of the phone calls I would have made today—"

"You'll run yourself ragged, Sara!"

She sighed, bowed her head and rubbed her temple, then looked back at him. "I don't have any choice, do I?"

The ensuing silence captured her attention. When he finally spoke, she was startled. "*I'll* go," Geoffrey stated emphatically. "You tell me where to go, whom to see, what to do and I'll do it. I can start at the hospital and see how your David's doing, then move on to the office. How about it?"

"I can't ask you to do that," she whispered, stunned.

Approaching her, he was the image of boldness. "You're not asking; I'm offering. I *want* to do it, Sara—unless you'd rather I didn't."

"I do want you to! I mean, it would make things so much easier. But what about *your* work? You've got enough to do—"

"It'll hold." He took her shoulders and drew her up. "Besides, it really is my turn."

"Your turn?"

"To do some of that traveling. It's got to be

hard on you, shuttling back and forth the way you do."

"I don't mind," she whispered, feeling ever so close to him.

"Well, I do," he countered. "But I'll only go to New York on one condition."

She slid her arms around his waist in mirror to his movement and tipped her head back. "What's that?"

"That you get some sleep. Early nights. Both nights."

"And what else would I do with you gone?" she burst out with soft spontaneity. When he lowered his head and kissed her, she wondered all the more.

"I don't know," he murmured against her lips, then caressed her cheek with slow kisses en route to her ear. "What did you do before?"

"I don't know," she breathed, her eyes closed, hypnotized by his nearness. When he held her like this, so gently, so strongly, she could think of nothing but the moment. It was a heady one, arms around one another, bodies snugly fitted. She drank in the clean male smell of him, let her hands slide higher to the broader span of his upper back. When he returned to her lips and kissed her again, she let her response speak wordlessly of her love.

"Know what I'd like to do?" he whispered in a hoarser tone.

"What?" she asked, as if the tensing of his body hadn't given him away.

"Take you back to bed."

"Right now?"

"Right now."

"Whose bed?" The question had popped out, seemingly, from a little gremlin perched on the shoulder of her heart. It was as close as she could come to asking if Jeff loved her. But just as her heart waited anxiously, the door to the kitchen swung open and Mrs. Fleming came in.

"Oh! Excuse me—" she exclaimed, disappearing as quickly. But both heads had swung her way, and the spell was broken.

"Well . . . uh . . ." Geoffrey slowly released Sara and stood back. "I guess I'd better call the office, then the airport to see what they've got flying out today. If you could make some notes as to what I can do for you, it'd be a big help."

Sara nodded, unable to say a word. She'd come so close to knowing; it seemed unfair. But as though to compensate for the disappointment, there was the knowledge of that other burden Geoffrey had lifted from her shoulders. Following him to the library, she realized that only half of her relief came from not having to make the trip. The other half came from knowing that her husband was doing this for her. And the question would have another chance to be answered one day.

For Geoffrey the trip from San Francisco to New York was an eye-opener. He'd expected four and a half hours of relaxation, but he brooded the entire time. Did she love him? Did she not? For the first time he could appreciate the advantage of being back in San Francisco, busy and running all the time except when he was with her. If *he* had to make this trip twice a week, he'd lose his mind—unless, that was, he knew that she loved him and was waiting for him—better still, was with him during the flight. That might be fun, he mused. Perhaps even for this benefit of hers . . . perhaps he'd go back with her then. After all, between Caryn and Mrs. Fleming, Lizzie would be doted on, and Sara did need an escort.

She was remarkable, he decided at the start of his second Scotch. She'd arranged the party—food, seating, flowers and wine and song. Where *had* she found that small wood-wind ensemble? For that matter, where had she found those other resources? Everyone seemed to come when she called, and she seemed perfectly comfortable dealing with them all. It was a switch from the past, to say the least. Then she'd had all she could do simply to psych herself for the event; she'd been more than happy to leave the arrangements to others. In fact, when he'd first suggested the party, he'd assumed she'd let Mrs. Fleming handle almost everything. Now, though, not only had Sara taken the details upon herself, but she'd managed to make Mrs. Fleming feel like a million by convincing her that her role of overseeing the others was vital, when in truth it was a token one.

Yes, Sara was a wonder. She was also worn out. He could see it in her pallor, in the way she often dozed against him in the evenings, in the sunken cast to her eyes before she'd dusted them with makeup. She was pushing herself far beyond the call of duty, and he didn't know why. Did she love him? Or was she simply carrying out her part of the bargain with a characteristic thoroughness? He was back to square one. Perhaps it was time for another Scotch.

A stewardess came from behind and passed his seat, looking calmly from left to right in search of passengers in need of help. Geoffrey started to call her, then dropped his hand and simply watched the slender blond move out of reach. There had been a time when he might have made a pass at such an attractive woman. No longer. Only one woman interested him now.

His eyes dropped to the gold band on his finger and he noted how comfortable it felt. *She* was comfortable. The marriage itself was comfortable. If only he knew what the future held. If only he could freely confess his love. But that might be pushing her. If she balked at a vow that implied deeper involvement, he'd be all the more frustrated. Besides, would she even believe him? They'd been in love before, and he'd let things come between them. What good were words of love? Better to show her.

A wry smile tugged at his lips as he recalled his plan to keep cool, to hold her at arm's length. Had he really thought it possible, or had he merely been too cowardly to admit the truth—that Sara intrigued him even more now than she had ten years ago in Snowmass? It was in the image of man to think himself strong and in full control of his destiny. But was he? Where Sara was involved, he felt helpless.

* * *

Sara, on the other hand, was far from helpless. Geoffrey saw it everywhere he turned in New York, hearing her praises sung by her co-workers, seeing the efficient operation of Sara McCray Originals for himself. Even with David confined to the hospital for what had been diagnosed as a mercifully mild heart attack, the business was in fine shape. It didn't take Geoffrey long to realize that the buoyant welcome he received was simply the overspill of an adoration that was aimed at his wife rather than a dire relief that help had arrived. For many another man it might have been a demoralizing experience to ride on his wife's coattails. For Jeff, however, self-confident and successful as he was on his own, it was an occasion for pride that was to continue that Saturday night at the party she'd so skillfully arranged. It was an unqualified success. The food was superb, the setting elegant, the air one of pleasured luxuriance. The consummate hostess, Sara moved from group to group, exuding genuine warmth, joining ongoing conversation, fully enjoying herself and her coup.

Geoffrey's astonishment at the evening's achievement was tempered only by his attentiveness. He was always there to introduce her to newcomers, always there to push Sara McCray Originals when her own modesty quieted her, always there to see that she was in want of neither food nor drink. Though he circulated on his own as was his obligation as host, he always returned to her side, to be rewarded when she reached out and took his hand or arm to draw him into the circle.

She was the perfect wife and hostess, until the last of the guests, the last of the help, had left and she collapsed into a chair in utter exhaustion. For Geoffrey, having spent the evening in near-worship of her, his worry took a harsher note than it might have done in more normal circumstances.

"Damn it, Sara! I knew you shouldn't have done all this! You look like you can't take another step!"

"I can't." She laughed wearily, looking up at him. "But I don't have to until tomorrow—uh, make that today."

His gaze narrowed darkly. "You're not going to—"

"I have to," she said with a sigh. "There's still so much to do for the benefit. I've got to speak with the designers and check on the progress of the work." She shook her head. "I was hoping to stay here until Thursday, but with David still out of commission, I'd better get back on Wednesday. If things are actually going to be done by Friday night—"

"If you don't slow down, y*ou'll* be the one in the hospital, not David. Then where will we be?" he exclaimed impulsively, knowing how much he'd come to depend on her presence yet speaking without thought of the possible interpretation of his words—or misinterpretation.

Stiffening, Sara pushed herself from the chair and headed for the stairs, all her joy gone. She was, as she saw it, no different to Jeff than those caterers or florists or musicians had been to her tonight. She served one purpose above all others. "Don't worry," she seethed. "I'll be fine."

But she wasn't. And though she'd expected Geoffrey to be calm and forgiving by the next morning, he wasn't. Sunday, Monday and Tuesday were tense. By the time Wednesday barreled in and she boarded a plane headed for New York, she was drained not only physically but emotionally.

It was some help when the demands of the upcoming benefit diverted her thoughts from the worst of her brooding. But then there was the issue of her physical exhaustion, the solution to which would only have given her time to think—and that she didn't want. So she kept herself moving, doing even more than she'd planned, telling herself that she'd rest when the benefit was over. By the time Geoffrey arrived, she was running on fumes.

"Geoffrey? *Here*?" she squawked back at the receptionist when the message arrived at midafternoon. When the man himself appeared at the door to her office, an answer was unnecessary. Murmuring a stunned "Thank you," she hung up the phone and stood, her heart pounding, unable to take her eyes from the tall, dark vision before her. "Jeff! When did you fly in?" Though he looked incredibly formal, he no longer seemed angry.

"I came straight from the airport," he explained, studying her intently. His half-smile held no humor at all. "I figured I ought to witness firsthand this affair that's taken so much out of you."

"I'm fine. Really fine." Certainly better, knowing that he'd thought to come—indeed, one part of her was ecstatic that he'd made the effort to fly all the way to New York after having flown round-trip just the week before. It would pick her up to have him here, and at the moment she badly needed a pick-me-up. She smiled wearily. "I'll be glad when it's over, though. I can't remember when anything like this has been as tiring."

His eyes narrowed in hint of his earlier anger. "Maybe that's because you've never worn as many hats before. Has it occurred to you that you may be overdoing it?"

"What can I do, Jeff? I didn't plan to have everything come at once. For that matter, I agreed to do this benefit over a year ago. I had no idea then that I'd be shuttling from coast to coast now!" Her voice had risen in accusation and anger. It seemed they were picking up the argument where they'd last left off. But she was neither prepared for that particular pain nor particularly well tuned to handle it. "Look," she said with a sigh, "you're right. I'm exhausted. And the last thing I need is to argue with you." She glanced down at her watch. "I've got another hour's work to do here before I go home to change. If you want, you can wait—"

But he shook his head and took his topcoat from his arm in prelude to donning it. "I've got an errand to run. What time do you have to be at the hotel?"

"Six."

"I'll pick you up at five forty-five. Okay?"

"Okay."

By the evening's end Sara was convinced she had a guardian angel. Not only did the benefit net a quarter of a million dollars in aid to handicapped children, but, in the limelight, her jewelry looked even more stupendous than she'd hoped. And Geoffrey was with her, a handsome and dignified escort, attracting more than his share of speculative glances. As a couple, they were stunning, he in his black tuxedo, she in her floor-length gown of softly draped red chiffon. He complemented her perfectly in every way, carrying the heaviest burden of conversation each time she began to fade, dropping into the background when the moment's rest revived her. His was a strong arm to lean on, a quiet presence to give her strength.

When he took her home to her apartment that night, she was optimistic. When they made feverish love to one another into the early morning hours, she was ecstatic. When the phone rang at nine the next morning, though, waking them both from the sleep she, for one, so badly needed, she felt instantly on guard.

Groping blindly, she found the receiver and cleared her throat as she brought it to her ear. "Hello? Yes?" Her voice cleared instantly. "Mrs. Fleming?" The warm length of man beside her shifted. When a long arm reached for the phone, she twisted and hung on determinedly. "That's all right. We had to get up anyway. Is something wrong?" As she listened to the San Francisco connection, her eyes widened in alarm. "When did it start? Any fever? Uh-oh. And that didn't bring it down?"

"What is it?" Geoffrey demanded against her free ear, but she held a hand up for him to wait and gave her full attention to Mrs. Fleming.

"Did you put in a call to Dr. Shaw? I know, but her answering service will contact her."

"Sara—"

Sitting up on the side of the bed now, she ignored both her nudity and her husband's urgent tone. "No, no, Mrs. Fleming. You've done the right thing." She squinted at the clock across the room. "I tell you what—why don't you call and leave word for the doctor while I call the airport and try to get an earlier flight out. I'll get back to you within the hour. Okay?" After one or two final words she hung up the phone to face a duly concerned Geoffrey.

"What's wrong? It's Lizzie, isn't it?"

"She got sick yesterday afternoon and had a bad night."

"Sick? What kind of sick?"

"Fussing and fever: Her stomach's not holding much." Sara's face held a world of worry. "I'd like to take the first flight possible." But Geoffrey was one step ahead, sprawling across her to grab the phone. Within minutes they were booked on a ten-fifty flight, scrambling to shower, dress and pack before calling a cab.

The flight seemed endless for them both. Sitting side by side, they said barely a word, each wallowing in worry and guilt. By the time Cyrus met them in San Francisco, they were both in ill humor. By the time they arrived at the house, ill humor had taken a backseat to raw tension.

"How is she?" Sara asked, bounding through the door and quickly shrugging out of her coat.

Mrs. Fleming was there to greet them. "About the same. The doctor did stop by, though. She feels it's nothing more than a stomach bug. But my heart goes out for the little thing. She just wants to be held."

Geoffrey had already started up the stairs. Squeezing Mrs. Fleming's arm in silent thanks, Sara went after him. They reached Lizzie's room moments later to find the child being rocked in Caryn's arms. Geoffrey took her quickly.

"And what's the matter with you, pumpkin?" he crooned, smoothing her hair from her forehead and kissing its warmth. Her tiny cheeks were pale, her eyes had a fevered sheen, her lower lip quivered. And before he could murmur another word, she held her small arms out to Sara.

"Mommeeee ... Mommeee," she whimpered, quieting only when Sara had taken her and held her close.

"There, sweetheart, it's all right. Mommy's here." Cuddling the child, she turned and sank into the rocker Caryn had vacated. "Mommy's here."

Mommy was there for the better part of the next three days, napping only when Lizzie did and even then with one eye open in case the warm Jell-O that had been victoriously coaxed down decided to make the return trip on its own.

"Let me sit with her awhile," Geoffrey urged time and again, but Sara's response was always the same.

"She's comfortable now. It's all right."

"But what about you? You haven't gotten any rest."

"I'm okay. She seems a little better. I'll relax when the fever's finally down."

When that time came Sara was in nearly as depleted a state as the child. She slept around the clock, then on and off for another day. When she still felt weak, Geoffrey took things into his own hands.

"You've *what*?" she asked, having woken from a nap to find Geoffrey in the chair by her bed, staring at her darkly.

"I've asked Tom Royce to stop by. I want him to take a look at you."

"There's nothing wrong with me, Jeff! I only need some rest."

"You've had two days of rest and you're still not yourself. Lizzie's already made up for lost time and then some. Not you."

"She's a child. Children bounce back much faster. Besides, I'm sure I've just got a touch of whatever it was she had. And on top of being run down, it's no wonder I'm still tired."

"You're not eating."

"I'm not hungry." The very thought of food made her sick.

"But how can you regain your strength without eating?"

Drained, she settled deeper into the pillows and closed her eyes. "I'll eat tomorrow."

"In the meantime I'll feel more comfortable with a doctor's opinion."

Her eyes flew open and she would have protested, but he was out of his seat, at the door and gone before she could muster the strength. Perhaps he was right, she mused. Besides, what harm was there in a simple doctor's visit?

She was to have severe second thoughts several hours later, though, when Tom Royce closed his bag and looked at her from his perch on her bedside. "You're run down. There's no doubt about that."

They were interrupted by a soft knock on the door. When Geoffrey poked his head in and saw that the worst of the examination was over, he came to stand by the bed. "Well?"

"I was just telling your wife that she is definitely run down." He looked back at Sara. "But I doubt you have what the child had. There's no fever, no vomiting." He hesitated, looked toward Geoffrey, then back. "Is there any chance that you're pregnant?"

"Pregnant?" Sara's eyes widened and her face grew all the more pale. "No. I'm not pregnant."

Geoffrey had stiffened. "My wife takes ample precaution against that," he gritted.

Ignoring his caustic tone, the doctor turned to Sara. "What do you take?"

"Take?" she echoed dumbly.

"Birth control pills. That *was* what Jeff meant, wasn't it?"

"Uh . . ." She shot a fearful glance at her husband and considered lying. But she'd come too far in life to resort to that. "Uh, yes, but no . . ."

Geoffrey paled. "No, what?" His voice was low and taut, hers little more than a whisper when she answered.

"No, I'm not taking anything."

An enigmatic light flashed in his eyes. *"Nothing?"* he exclaimed, every cell in his body seeming to come to attention. "Then you really might be pregnant?"

"I'm not!" she countered, the doctor quite forgotten.

Geoffrey frowned, seeming irritated. "How do you know?"

"I *know*. That's all."

Tom Royce leaned forward. "When was the last time you saw your gynecologist, Sara?"

She turned to him, stunned. "I—uh—it was last summer."

"When was your last period?"

For several seconds she sat so still that the thunderous beat of her heart seemed to shake her slender body. Again she looked at Geoffrey; again she looked back. "I'm not sure. Things . . . things have been so busy. I guess I've lost track."

There was no question about Geoffrey's irritation now. It was very real, indeed verging on the angry. "What kind of story is that? You're so damned efficient in every other thing, and you expect me to believe that you can't keep track of something as simple—"

"It's inconsequential!"

"Not if you might be pregnant!

"But I'm not!"

The doctor patted her arm. "Calm down," he said as he shot a glance over his shoulder. "Both of you. I think it would be a good idea to see a doctor anyway. You'll need to have some blood tests and my guess is a hefty prescription of vitamins. As for the other, whoever you see

283

can settle the matter. If you'd like, I'll call your doctor and tell him about our visit."

Sara forced a quick smile. "That's all right. He's in New York. When I'm back there next week—"

"No way!" Geoffrey returned to the fray, his eyes alight with fury. "You'll see someone *here. This* week." He turned to his friend. "Who's the best?"

The doctor took a prescription pad and a pen from his jacket pocket and proceeded to scrawl a name. Obviously agreeing with Geoffrey's firm stance, he tore off the sheet of paper and, bypassing Sara, handed it to him.

Sara was livid, which didn't help her state. Nor did another night's restless sleep. She was still seething when Geoffrey hustled her into the office of a top OB-GYN man the next morning. She knew her anger was a defense mechanism, a cover-up for hope and fear and an intense case of confusion. And for that the doctor had no medicine, as she was quickly to learn with the pronouncement of his diagnosis.

Ten

"**Y**ou certainly are pregnant," he declared before Sara had even risen from the examining table. Lending a hand, he helped her sit up.

"You're sure?" she whispered.

The doctor's kind smile was a futile attempt to ease her evident tension. "I've been in this business for far too long to miss the most obvious signs. Between what you've told me and what I just saw, I'd say you've entered your third month." He paused, gently puzzled. "What I don't understand is why you didn't suspect it sooner."

"I didn't suspect it at all!" she returned,

shock rounding her brown eyes all the more.

"You're young, newly married. You weren't using any form of birth control. Surely you were aware that it might happen."

"But I wasn't!" She eyed the doctor in helpless confusion. "I can't be pregnant. They told me—"

"*Who* told you?"

"The doctor who did the surgery."

"Whoa. I think I'm missing something." He leaned back against the edge of the examining table and rubbed his jaw. "You didn't say anything out there about surgery other than a routine appendectomy."

"*You* said routine. I said appendectomy."

"Then it was more?"

She looked down at her clenched hands. "Yes. Well, it started as an appendectomy, with pains and all. But in the process of the operation they found a cluster of ovarian cysts. By the time they were done, I was left with barely half an ovary." Distressed, she looked up. "I was fifteen at the time. They told me the chances were very slim that I'd ever become pregnant. It was devastating." She hesitated, glancing toward the closed door, beyond which her husband sat. "Geoffrey just assumed I'd been taking something. I . . . I didn't have the courage to set him straight."

The doctor studied her closely. "You are pleased about the baby, aren't you?"

It was the question of the day. Oh, yes, she was pleased. Thrilled, ecstatic! But what about Jeff, and what of their bargain? The fact of a child would inevitably alter things. But how? For better or for worse?

"I—I think so." She smiled weakly. "It's so sudden. I can't quite believe it."

"Oh, you can believe it, Sara. Take my word." Standing forward, he took a deep breath. "Well, now, why don't you get dressed. I'll go give your husband the good news, then I want to sit down and talk with you both. I'm sure there will be questions you'll want to ask."

The questions Sara wanted to ask were not of the doctor but of Geoffrey. But he was intent on questioning the doctor, as he'd already begun to do before she appeared, pale and hesitant, at the examining room door. The doctor's expression was by far the less forbidding of the two to greet her.

"Have a seat, Sara. Geoffrey was just asking how long this fatigue you've been experiencing will last."

Preoccupied with trying to analyze Geoffrey's tone, his expression, the utter control of his body as he sat next to her, she barely heard a word, managing simply to nod at the appropriate places and offer an intermittent yes or uh-huh. Reluctant to make an already tenuous situation worse, she let him pocket her vitamin prescription, arrange for her next appointment, usher her to the car and drive her home. It was only when they'd entered the front hall that he turned to her, his expression grim and his voice hard.

"Full bed rest for two days. That was what he said. You go on upstairs. I'll call New York."

"I can—"

"*I'll* do it." His eyes flashed in anger, squelching her protest. Then he turned his back on her and disappeared into the library, closing the doors behind him with an eloquent thud.

Sara had not the wish, much less the strength, to call him back. Turning, she headed for bed, only to find that rest was elusive while her emotional turmoil raged. She needed to think, to ingest it all, to reorder the priorities in her life, allowing for this element that had so miraculously entered it.

Rising, she threw on a pair of jeans and a sweater and sought refuge in the solarium with the plants and her thoughts. Geoffrey was angry. She knew it. He hadn't bargained for a child when he'd asked her to marry him. And now he'd have another responsibility, one that would far exceed the time limit they'd set.

Pressing her fingers to her lips, she felt the burden of that responsibility herself. Then, quite spontaneously, she grew indignant. What had he expected? He'd never asked; he had simply assumed she'd seen to the matter of birth control. But what about *him*? It was a responsibility fully shared; his had been as active a role as hers in the accomplishment.

For the first time since Tom Royce had uttered the word *pregnant* the day before, a tentative smile gentled Sara's features. She was pregnant, actually pregnant! After living nearly half her life assuming its impossibility, she was pregnant! And with Geoffrey's child— what thought could be more beautiful!

There was one—that Geoffrey might love her—but she dismissed it as improbable. Oh, yes, he'd be more than willing to look after her and the baby. After all, there was still Lizzie, who needed a mother. What better way to secure Sara's services indefinitely? Not that it was an unpleasant picture. To the contrary. The thought of the four of them together—she and Jeff, Lizzie and a new baby—made her glow. But while one part of her felt she'd been given the greatest gift of all, the other part was terrified of what life would be like living with Geoffrey in a state of constant antagonism. She'd been through it once before, and baby or no baby, she doubted she could do it again. She was her own woman now. If need be she would raise the baby alone.

"I thought I told you to go to bed!" came a furious outburst from the direction of the door. Sara whirled to find Geoffrey closing in on her with an air of imperiousness that easily ignited her own temper. It was time to take a stand at last.

"And I didn't want to just then," she returned, tipping her chin up in defiance.

"You heard what the doctor said: complete bed rest."

"And you were the one who said, 'Fine, doctor.' If you're so determined to obey him, *you* go to bed. I'll do what I please." Having expended this token bit of rebellion, she felt strangely relieved. Or was she simply buoyed by the glimmer of surprise that her strident tone brought to Geoffrey's eye? She watched him draw himself up before her, pace to the far side of the solarium, turn and study her from there, then slowly walk back. She stood boldly, refusing to look away, knowing she had nothing to lose by holding firm. It was about time they started being honest with one another. And at that moment she didn't care to be ordered around.

She didn't know what she expected—perhaps further argument, perhaps his terse exit. What she didn't expect was the sudden softening of his features. Nor, when he spoke, was she prepared for his words.

"I guess I owe you an apology, Sara," he began quietly, standing directly before her with his hands thrust deep in his pockets. "You really didn't ask for any of this. You didn't want any of it. *I* was the one who got you into it, and I realize that I've caused you all kinds of trouble."

When he paused, Sara held her breath. Not only did she not know what to say, but she sensed something else coming, something more momentous than an apology. His expression was like none she'd ever seen him wear—a blend of strength and humility, simultaneously innocent yet knowing. Strangely, she felt his business associates would have seen him this way. That was it. He seemed to be bargaining once more, though far differently than he'd done back in November. Looking up at him, she waited to hear his offer.

"I've given this much thought," he continued evenly. "In light of what's happened, I feel it only fair to offer you your freedom." He ignored her blanching. "It's obviously an unfair strain on you, having to go back and forth to New York, and I could never ask you to give up your business. After all, you are first and foremost Sara McCray, and that's how it should be. You're every bit as devoted to your company as my mother was to hers."

The rising heat of anger simmered within Sara. Her fists clenched at her sides and her eyes wide with disbelief, she would have spoken up had not Geoffrey gone calmly, coolly on.

"I'll give you whatever you want, Sara. Of course, there will be a generous settlement for you, and if you decide to go ahead and have the child—"

"If I decide . . . ?" she whispered in dismay.

He was unfazed. "If you decide to go ahead and have the child, I'll certainly support it. In fact, if you should choose to give birth but find that a baby interferes with your life in New York, I'll be glad to take custody of it. I'd be generous with visitation rights."

"Visitation rights?" She mouthed the words, unable at first to comprehend them. Was this Geoffrey talking, discussing a divorce in such a dispassionate tone, systematically tossing out suggestions for the disposal of an as-yet-unborn child? Had it *all* been a farce—the warm hours they'd spent together, the gentle looks, the lovemaking? Could he dismiss her just like that?

"I don't believe you," she murmured, her knees trembling in time with her insides. "I don't believe you!"

"I'm serious," he insisted, goading her with his amicability. "Your life has been turned upside down, and it's my fault. I'll do whatever you want to try to right things." He paused, his gaze searing. "You know how much I've wanted a child . . . but I'm willing to make the arrangements should you decide to have an abortion."

"An abortion?" Her voice was hoarse, then stronger the second time out. "An *abortion*?" She was shaking from head to toe now, positively livid. She took a blind step back, feeling chilled even as she burned. "I don't want an *abortion*! And I don't want a divorce!" After all he'd done, he was trying to dump her. She'd never in her life been so enraged. Stalking forward again, she jabbed his chest with a finger.

"For your information, you're in this up to your ears. And I have no intention whatsoever of letting you off the hook!" Her voice rose half an octave. "Just who do you think you are, that you can play with people's lives this way? Just because you've always had everything you've wanted doesn't mean it's right! And don't you ever, *ever* compare me to your mother! Your mother was a ruthless woman without a drop of warmth in her. So long as I live, I pray to be more human!" Exasperated, she threw her hands into the air, started to walk away, then turned back, thrust her hands on her hips and resumed her tirade. "I should have expected it. I should have known. You did it once before— let me go just as you'd dismiss the hired help." She took a breath to steady herself but it seemed futile. Fury had become her master.

"Well, you won't do it this time, Geoffrey! I'm not being let go so easily! This time you'll have to *kick* me out. And I'm warning you, you'll have a fight on your hands." She stared at him hard. "I won't be bought off. I don't need your money! Nor does my child. But I'll have a husband and a father for my baby. And I'll be a mother to Lizzie"—her eyes narrowed, her voice lowered in challenge—"until the day you can prove I'm unfit."

The strain of the outpouring began to take its toll. Pausing momentarily, Sara felt as stunned by her own words as by those that had incited them. Her eyes grew more sad, her cheeks more pale. "Because I'm a good mother, Jeff. I love Lizzie. And I'll love this baby, too. And regardless of what you say, I'm proud of myself for having juggled family and career, having done what I've done."

Her emotions were fast overcoming her. Looking down, she studied the marble floor, but its graceful whorls offered no solace. When she looked back up and spoke, her voice was wrenched deep from her soul. "I didn't need to marry you to open a West Coast branch. I have sufficient funds *and* sufficient contacts. Surely you knew that." She faltered but went on. "Why do you think I *did* agree to the marriage, if not to add something to my life that was missing? We had some pretty high hopes once. Don't you think I wanted to see if we could recapture what we'd lost?" Her eyes misted, and her voice dropped to a whisper. "Didn't it occur to you that I might—that I might fall in love with you again?"

Hearing the words, she was furious at herself—furious for having fallen in love, furious for having confessed to it. Unable to see Geoffrey's face through her tears, she clutched at the tattered shreds of her pride. "I'll tell you one thing. Now that I've finally found what I need to make my life complete, I'm *not* letting go! You've done such a fine job playing at love for the past two months . . . and you can damn well keep it up!"

Whirling to make her exit on a note of dignity, she strode across the floor and reached for the door, only to find it locked. She jiggled the knob and pulled, jiggled and pulled again, but it wouldn't give. Turning back, she caught sight of the smug smile on Geoffrey's face. And with a moment's insight she realized that Geoffrey must have tripped the button to lock the door, realized that he'd wanted to keep her in, realized that he hadn't had any intention of letting her go as he'd said, realized that she'd taken the bait just as he'd intended.

"You called my bluff," she cried in dismay.

Geoffrey slowly approached. "You bet I did.

And it worked." With the broadening of his smile, his dimple taunted her mercilessly. "It's about time one of us blurted it all out. I simply gave you a push."

"You took advantage of me when I was down," she accused, but her indignation was forced. In truth, she didn't know whether to be angry or relieved. "That's not fair! I'm in no shape to handle your sly maneuvering!"

"Lady, what with that little demonstration you just gave, I think you're in perfect shape for what I have in mind." Without another word he pulled her into his arms and kissed her long and hard in a firm statement of possession. When he released her at last, they were both breathless.

Yet nothing had been resolved in Sara's mind save the fact that he still found her attractive. If need be she could always withhold *that*. "And what about you, Jeff?" she asked, drawing back from the circle of his arms. "Tell me something I *don't* know."

He looked down at her then, his features fierce in a tender kind of way. "I love you, Sara. I want you here with me forever. I *need* you. Can't you see that?"

Hearing the urgent ring to his tone, she allowed for cautious hope. "I want to see it, but

I . . . it's sometimes hard. There are times when you seem so distant, when I don't know what you're thinking, when I'm afraid to tell you what *I'm* thinking."

"We don't talk."

She dared a tiny smile. "You mean, we talk—but we don't talk."

"Exactly. And that's what we're going to have to change. From now on, what's on the mind is on the tongue."

"I love you," she whispered in instant obedience.

"And I love you," he returned, only then holding out his arms in the invitation she'd been waiting for. Without hesitation she melted against him, exhausted but exuberant. "This is where you belong," he vowed. "Never forget it." He crushed her to him then, burying his face in her golden hair. "I love you, Sara McCray Parker. I love you."

Sara had never heard words more glorious. "Do you really?" she asked, struggling to accept that her hopes might be fulfilled.

"Oh, yes," he moaned with a shudder. "I love you." They stood together then, hugging one another in expression of their hearts' desire. When Geoffrey moved at last, it was only to lift her into his arms and carry her to the door. "The key," he whispered hoarsely. "In the pocket of my shirt."

Fumbling, Sara dug it out at last, pausing along the way to plant warm kisses beneath his open collar. His skin seemed suddenly all the more beckoning. "How long would you have kept me locked up?"

"Until you decided to stay."

She held the key up before him. "I gave in pretty quick, huh?"

He gave her an adoring glance. "Pretty quick." Then he cocked his head toward the door. "Open it."

"What if I don't? There are two sides to every game, you know. I can remember one interesting night we spent right here."

"Open the door," he growled.

She reached down and did so. "Where are you taking me?"

"Just following doctor's orders."

"Doctor's orders?"

"Uh-huh. He ordered bed rest and that's just what you're going to get."

"But Jeff—"

"Don't argue."

She didn't. For it was his bed to which he carried her—his bed, at last.

* * *

She was still there two days later when Geoffrey burst in, his face alight with the same love in which she'd basked ever since. Leaning over, he kissed her gently, lingeringly, then stood to shrug out of his jacket and toss it on a chair.

"You're home early," she remarked in delight as she laid her sketch pad on the nightstand.

He grinned endearingly. "I couldn't seem to concentrate." Then he craned his neck to tug at the knot of his tie. "Funny, but that seems to be a perpetual problem lately."

"Oh?"

"Don't you *oh* me with such innocence. I'm sure you know precisely what the problem is." His tie fell atop the jacket, and he went to work on the buttons of his shirt. Sara watched entranced, aware of her growing arousal as he undressed. When he stepped out of his pants, he finally spoke. "Okay, let's have it. What's on that mind of yours right now?"

"Right now? I was thinking how much I adore your body." Sliding from beneath the covers, she knelt on the bed and reached out to him. He came eagerly, falling back to the mattress with her, cushioning her tenderly. They lay then with their arms and legs entwined, their faces mere inches from one another. Sara tipped her head back, resting it on the corded swell of his shoulder. "It's very exciting."

"Is that so?" he asked, his eyes gleaming naughtily.

"Uh-huh."

He kissed her once, very gently, then smoothed a long strand of hair from her cheek and grew serious. "Did I ever tell you why I waited until I was twenty-eight to marry?"

"I assumed it was because you had everything you wanted without marriage. That was one of the things that bothered me most when things got tough. I kept asking myself why you married me when you'd had all those other, more sophisticated women at your beck and call."

"I didn't want them, Sara. I only wanted you. You were the one who had the warmth I needed. You were different. You were alive. And you still are all those things and more. Oh!" Pulling from her grasp, he jumped from the bed.

"Geoffrey, where—"

"You get me so crazy, woman, that I can't think straight! There *was* a purpose—uh, excuse me, *another* purpose—for my coming home early." Leaning over the chair, he dug into his jacket pocket to remove a small box wrapped in white paper held by a slim satin ribbon.

"What's this for?" Sara asked, eyeing the box as he handed it to her.

"This is just . . . because."

"Just because?"

He smiled roguishly. "Just because. Go on. Open it."

With a dubious glance his way, she carefully untied the ribbon and removed the paper to reveal, as she'd suspected, a ring box. Lifting its lid, though, she gasped.

"Geoffrey . . . what . . . ?" Reaching in gently, she lifted an exquisite uncut diamond from inside. Turning it gingerly, she studied it from every angle, her jeweler's eye easily understanding its worth. "It's magnificent. But I don't understand . . ."

"It's for you, Sara. I want you to design a ring for yourself."

"But I've never worked with diamonds."

"So I noticed. But why not? You work with rubies, sapphires and emeralds. Why not diamonds?"

"Because . . . because . . ."

"Honestly."

"Honestly? Because, in my mind, diamonds have always been synonymous with engagement rings and promises of happiness."

"And you thought you'd never have one?"

"I guess not."

"Well, you're wrong. This is it."

"But we're not—we've never been engaged."

"No," he conceded, gently confident. "This ring is my way of saying thanks."

"For what?" she asked more shyly.

"For being you. For loving me. For taking Lizzie into your heart." He slid a knowing hand down to her stomach. "For offering me the promise of a child."

Choked, she closed one hand around the diamond and with her other reached to draw his hand from her stomach to her cheek. "I still can't believe I'm pregnant," she whispered falteringly. "I thought for so long—"

Taking her into his arms, Geoffrey held her tight. "When I stop to think of your living alone with that fear all this time, I ache inside. It wasn't fair, Sara. I loved you. I deserved to share that with you. And if you'd told me, we might have avoided at least one misunderstanding."

"I was so young, Jeff. I felt inadequate from the moment I entered this house. To tell you, on top of everything else, that I couldn't have a child—I just couldn't!"

"But look at you." He beamed. "I wouldn't exactly call you inadequate. And besides, even back then I loved you for *you*, not for what you could or could not do." Looking down at her upturned face, he placed soft kisses on each of her eyes in turn, then the tip of her nose and finally her lips. The sentiment went far beyond passion to a higher, sweeter emotion. When he drew back it was to uncurl her fingers gently and raise the diamond to the light. He stared at it, turned it, finally sprawled over her to set it carefully on the nightstand. Then he wound his fingers through Sara's hair and caressed her cheeks with his thumbs.

"Do you remember that first discussion we had about gemstones?" he asked softly. "We were in the cottage, up in your workshop, and I asked you about your favorites. You talked of those precious gems that were the most brilliant and colorful. And unique. That was what you said. Do you remember?"

"Yes," she whispered.

"Well, you know something? *You're* more

precious than any of them. You're brilliant and colorful. And you're unique. I don't think there's another person in the world with quite as many facets, every one sparkling and incomparable."

"Geoffrey," she chided softly, overjoyed yet embarrassed. "If you're not careful you'll give me as swelled a head as this stomach is going to be before long."

He sucked in his breath. "That will be beautiful." Then he lowered his head and kissed her with every bit of his heart and soul. "*You're* beautiful," he breathed against her lips. Before she could respond, his hands wandered to seek her out, skimming her breasts and her waist and hips, then retracing the path as though to define the whole of her and thereby make her real.

For Sara, too, it was a time of discovery. In the light of day she noted every shade, every contour of Geoffrey's body. She watched him, studied him, followed her hands and lips as they charted his virility. She found favored spots to adore—the soft mat of his chest just below his collarbone, the smooth, paler patch by his hip, the throbbing pulse at his neck made more so by her very exploration. It was a heady thought, the knowledge that she could arouse this man to a most ripe, most promising state, and she savored it as much as her own fast-rising state would allow.

When Geoffrey moved above her, she eagerly shifted to welcome him. His skin was hot against hers, creating a sensual friction that seared her thighs. He kissed her once more, with his tongue and his lips. Then, watching the love play in her eyes, he entered her.

"Ahhhhh. Oh, Jeff . . ."

"I know, princess. I know." For a minute he simply held her tight, needing the closeness, the full appreciation of what he'd found. Then he began to move in her, and clarity of thought yielded to the powerfully blinding force of love.

Nearby, a ray of sun broke through the drapes to fall across the diamond, a sparkling herald of the future.

An unforgettable story of love, loss
and rebuilding a life.

Barabara Delinsky's

A Woman Betrayed

Available now wherever books are sold.

The silence was deafening. Laura Frye sat in a corner of the leather sofa in the den, hugged her knees, and listened to it, minute after minute after minute. The wheeze of the heat through the vents couldn't pierce it. Nor could the slap of the rain on the windows, or the rhythmic tick of the small ship's clock on the shelf behind the desk.

It was five in the morning, and her husband still wasn't home. He hadn't called. He hadn't sent a message. His toothbrush was in the bathroom along with his razor, his after-shave, and the sterling comb and brush set Laura had given him for their twentieth anniversary the summer before. The contents of his closet were intact, right down to the small duffel he took with him to the sports club every Monday, Wednesday, and Friday. If he had slept somewhere else, he was totally ill equipped, which wasn't like Jeffrey at all, Laura knew. He was a precise man, a creature of habit. He never traveled, not for so much as a single night, without fresh underwear, a clean shirt, and a bar of deodorant soap.

More than that, he never went anywhere without telling Laura, and that was what frightened her most. She had no idea where he was or what had happened.

Not that she hadn't imagined. Laura wasn't usually prone to wild wanderings of the mind, but ten hours of waiting had taken its toll. She imagined that he'd had a stroke and lay unconscious across his desk in the deserted offices of Farro and Frye. She imagined that he'd been in an accident on the way home, that the car and everything in it had been burned beyond recognition or, alternately, that he had hit the windshield, climbed out, and begun wandering through the cold December rain not knowing who or where he was. She had gone so far as to imagine that he'd stopped for gas and had been taken hostage by a junkie holding up the nearby 7-Eleven.

More rational explanations for his absence had worn thin as night had waned. By no stretch of the imagination could she envision him holed up with a client at five in the morning. Maybe in April, with a new client whose tax records were in chaos but not the first week in December. And not without telling her. He always called if he was going to be late. Always.

Last night, they had been expected at an opening at the museum. Cherries had catered the affair. Though one of Laura's crews had handled the evening, she had spent the afternoon in Cherries' kitchen stuffing mushrooms, skewering smoked turkey and cherries, and cleaving baby lamb chops apart. She had wanted not only the food but the tables, the trays, and the bar to be perfect, which was why she had followed the truck to the museum to oversee the setting up.

Everything had been flawless. She had come home to change and get Jeff. But Jeff hadn't shown up.

Hugging her knees tighter in an attempt to fill the emptiness inside her, she stared at the phone. It had rung twice during the night. The first call had been from Elise, who was at the museum with her husband and wondered why Laura and Jeff weren't there. The second call had been from Donny for Debra, part of their nightly ritual. Sixteen-year-old sweethearts did that, Laura knew, just as surely as she knew that forty-something husbands who always called their wives if they were going to be late wouldn't not call unless something was wrong. So she had made several searching calls herself, but to no avail. The only thing she had learned was that the phone worked fine.

She willed it to ring now, willed Jeff to call and say he had had a late meeting with a client and had nearly fallen asleep at the wheel on the way home, so he'd pulled over to the side of the road to sleep off his fatigue. Of course, that wouldn't explain why the police hadn't spotted his car. Hampshire County wasn't so remote as to be without regular patrols or so seasoned as to take a shiny new Porsche for granted, particularly if that Porsche belonged to one half of a prominent Northampton couple.

The Frye name made the papers often, Jeff's with regard to the tax seminars he gave, Laura's with regard to Cherries. The local press was a tough one, seeming to resist anything upscale, which the restaurant definitely was, but Laura fed enough luminaries on a regular basis to earn frequent mentions. *State Senator DiMento and his entourage were seen debating ways to trim fat from the budget over steamed vegetables and salads at Cherries this week*, wrote Duggan O'Neil of the *Hampshire County Sun*. Duggan O'Neil could cut people to shreds, and he had done his share of cutting where Laura was concerned, but publicity was publicity, Jeff said. Name recognition was important.

Indeed, the police officer with whom Laura had talked earlier on the phone had known just who she was. He even remembered Jeff's car as the one often parked outside the restaurant. But nothing in his records suggested that anyone in the department had seen or heard of the black Porsche that night.

"Tell you what, Miz Frye," he had told her. "Since it's you, I'll make a few calls. Throw in a piece of cherry cheesecake, and I'll even call the state police." But his calls had turned up nothing, and, to her dismay, he had refused to let her file a missing persons report. "Not until he's been gone twenty-four hours."

"But awful things can happen in twenty-four hours!"

"Good things, too, like lost husbands coming home."

Lost husbands coming home. She resented those words with a passion. They suggested she was inept as a wife, inept as a woman, that Jeff had been bored and gone looking for fun and would wander back home when the fun was over. Maybe the cop lived that way, but not Jeff and Laura Frye. They had been together for twenty good years. They loved each other.

So where was he? The question gnawed at her. She imagined him slain by a hitchhiker, accosted by Satanists, sucked up, Porsche and all, by an alien starship. The possibilities were endless, each one more bizarre than the next. Bizarre things did happen, she knew, but to other people. Not to her. And not to Jeff. He was the most steadfast, the most predictable, the most uncorruptible man she'd ever known, which was why his absence made no sense at all.

Unfolding her legs, she rose from the sofa and padded barefoot through the dark living room to the front window. Drawing back the sheers that hung beneath full-length silk swags, she looked out. The wind was up, ruffling the branches of the pines, driving the rain against the flagstone walk and the tall lamp at its head.

At least it wasn't snowing. She remembered times, early in her marriage, when she had been home with the children during storms, waiting for Jeff to return from work. He had been a new CPA then, a struggling one, and they had lived in a rented duplex. Laura used to stand at the window, playing games with the children, drawing pictures on the glass in the fog their breath made. Like clockwork, Jeff had always come through the snow, barely giving her time to worry.

He worked in a new building in the center of town now, and they weren't living in the duplex, or even in that first weathered Victorian, but in a gracious brick Tudor on a tree-lined street, less than a ten minute drive from his office. It was a fast drive, an easy drive. But for some unknown and frightening reason he hadn't made it.

"Mom?"

Laura whirled around at the sudden sound to find Debra beneath the living room arch. Her eyes were sleepy, her dark hair disheveled. She wore a nightshirt with UMASS

COED NAKED LACROSSE splashed on the front over breasts that had taken a turn for the buxom in the past year.

Aware of her racing heart, Laura tried to smile. "Hi, Deb."

Debra sounded cross. "It's barely five. That's still the middle of the night, Mom. Why are you up?"

Unsure of what to say, just as she'd been unsure the night before when Debra had come home and Jeff hadn't been there, Laura threw back a gentle, "Why are you?"

"Because I woke up and remembered last night and started to worry. I mean, Dad's never late like that. I had a dream something awful happened, so I was going to check the garage and make sure the Porsche was—" Her voice stopped short. Her eyes probed Laura's in the dark. "It's there, isn't it?"

Laura shook her head.

"Where is he?"

She shrugged.

"Are you sure he didn't call and tell you something, and then you forgot? You're so busy, sometimes things slip your mind. Or maybe he left a message on the machine, but it got erased. Maybe he spent the night at Nana Lydia's."

Laura had considered that possibility, which was why she had driven past her mother-in-law's house when she had gone out looking for Jeff. In theory, Lydia might have taken ill and called her son, though in all likelihood she would have called Laura first. Laura was her primary caretaker. She was the one who stocked the house with food, took her to the doctor, arranged for the cleaning girl or the exterminator or the plumber.

"He's not there. I checked."

"How about the office?"

"I went there too." To the dismay of the guard, who had looked far more sleepy than Debra, she had insisted on checking the garage for the Porsche, but Jeff's space—the entire garage under his building—had been empty.

"Is he with David?"

"No. I called." David Farro was Jeff's partner, but he hadn't known of any late meetings Jeff might have had. Nor had Jeff's secretary, who had left at five with Jeff still in his office.

"Maybe with a client?"

"Maybe."

"But you were supposed to go to the museum. Wouldn't he have called if he couldn't make it?"

"I would have thought so."

"Maybe something's wrong with the phone."

"No."

"Maybe he had car trouble."

But he would have called, Laura knew. Or had someone call for him. Or the police would have seen him and called.

"So where is he?" Debra cried.

Laura was terrified by her own helplessness. "I don't know!"

"He has to be *somewhere*!"

She wrapped her arms around her middle. "Do you have any suggestions?"

"Me?" Debra shot back. "What do I know? You're the adult around here. Besides you're his wife. You're the one who knows him inside and out. You're supposed to know where he is." Turning back to the window, Laura drew the sheer aside and looked out again.

"Mom?"

"I don't know where he is, babe."

"Great. That's just great."

"No, it's not," Laura acknowledged, nervously scanning the street, "but there isn't an awful lot I can do right now. He'll show up, and I'm sure he'll have a perfectly good explanation for where he's been and why he hasn't called."

"If I ever stayed out all night without calling, you'd kill me."

"I may well kill your father," Laura said in a moment's burst of anger. Given what she'd been through, Jeff's explanation was going to have to be inspired if he hoped to be spared her fury. Then the fury died and fear returned. The possibilities flashed through her mind, one worse than the next. "He'll be home," she insisted, as much for her own sake as for Debra's.

"When?"

"Soon."

"How do you know?"

"I just know."

"What if he's sick, or hurt, or dying somewhere? What if he needs our help, but we're just standing here in a nice warm dry house waiting for him to show up? What if we're losing all this time when we should be out looking for him?"

Debra's questions weren't new. Laura had hit on all of them, more than once. Now she reasoned, "I looked for him last night. I drove around half the city and didn't see the Porsche. I called the police, and they hadn't seen it either. If there was an accident, the police would call me."

"So you're just going to stand here looking out the window? Aren't you *upset?*"

Debra was a sixteen-year-old asking a frightened sixteen-year-old's questions. Laura was a frightened thirty-eight-year-old with no answers, which made her frustration all the greater. Keeping her voice as steady as possible, given the tremulous feeling she had inside, she turned to Debra and said, "Yes, I'm upset. Believe me, I'm upset. I've been upset since seven o'clock last night, when your father was an hour late."

"He never does this, Mom, *never.*"

"I know that, Debra. I went to his office. I drove around looking for his car. I called his partner, his secretary, and the police, but they won't do anything until he's been gone a day, and he hasn't been gone half that. What would you have me do? Walk the streets in the rain, calling his name?"

Debra's glare cut through the darkness. "You don't have to be sarcastic."

With a sigh, Laura crossed the floor and caught her daughter's hand. "I'm not being sarcastic. But I'm worried, and your criticism doesn't help."

"I didn't criticize."

"You did." Debra said what was on her mind and always had. Disapproval coming from a little squirt of a child hadn't been so bad. Disapproval coming from someone who was Laura's own five-six and weighed the same one-fifteen, who regularly borrowed Laura's clothes, makeup, and perfume, who drove a car, professed to know how to French-kiss, and was physically capable of having a child of her own was something else. "You think I should be doing more than I am," Laura argued, "but I'm hamstrung, don't you see? I don't know if anything's really wrong. There could be a logical reason for your father's absence. I don't want to blow things out of proportion before I have good cause."

"Twelve hours isn't good cause?" Debra cried and whirled around to leave, only to be held back by Laura's grip.

"Eleven hours," she said with quiet control. "And, yes, it's good cause, babe. But I can't do anything right now but wait. I can't do anything else." The silence that followed was heavy with an unspoken plea for understanding.

Debra lowered her chin. Her hair fell forward, shielding her from Laura's gaze. "What about me? What am I supposed to do?"

Scooping the hair back from Debra's face, Laura tucked it behind an ear. For an instant she caught a glimpse of her daughter's worry, but it was gone by the time Debra raised her head. In its place was defiance. Taking that as part and parcel of the spunk that made Debra special, Laura said, "What you're supposed to do is go back to bed. It's too early to be up."

"Sure. Great idea. Like I'd really be able to sleep." She shot a glance at Laura's sweater and jeans. "Like you really slept yourself." She turned her head a fraction and gave a twitch of her nose. "You've been cooking, haven't you. What's that smell?"

"Borscht."

"Oh, gross."

"It's not so bad." Jeff loved it with sour cream on top. Maybe, deep inside, Laura had been hoping the smell would lure him home.

"I can't believe you were cooking."

"I always cook."

"At work. Not at home. Most of the time you stick us with Chunky Chicken Soup, Frozen French Bread Pizza, or Microwave Meatballs and Spaghetti. You must feel guilty that Dad's missing."

Laura ignored the suggestion, which could

have come straight from her own mother's an-
alytical mouth. "He isn't missing, just late."

"So you cooked all night."

"Not all night. Just part of it." In addition to
the borscht, she'd done a coq au vin she would
probably freeze, since no one planned to be
home for dinner for the next two nights. She
had also baked a Black Forest cake and two
batches of pillow cookies, one of which she
would send to Scott.

"Did you sleep at all?" Debra asked.

"A little."

"Aren't you tired?"

"Nah. I'm fine." She was too anxious to
sleep, which was why she had cooked. Nor-
mally, cooking relaxed her. It hadn't done that
last night, but at least it had kept her hands
busy.

"Well, I'm fine too," Debra declared. "I'll
shower and dress and sit down here with you."

Laura knew what was coming. Debra was
social to the core. Rarely did a weekend pass
when she wasn't out, if not with Donny, then
with Jenna or Kim or Whitney or all three and
more. But as drawn as she was to her friends,
she was allergic to anything academic. At the
slightest excuse, she would stay home for the

day. "You'll go to school when it's time," Laura insisted, "just like always."

"I can't go to school. I want to be here."

"There's nothing for you to do here. When your father comes home, he'll want to sleep."

"Assuming he hasn't already slept."

Laura felt a flare of indignance. "Where would he have slept?"

Debra's eyes went wide in innocence. "I don't know. Where do you think?"

"I don't know! If I did, we wouldn't be standing here at this hour discussing it!" Hearing the high pitch of her voice, Laura realized just how short-tempered she was—and how uncharacteristic that was. "Look," she said more calmly, "we're going in circles. I know nothing, you know nothing. All we can do for the time being is wait for your father to call. If I haven't heard from him by eight or nine, I can start making calls myself." Framing Debra's face with her hands, she said, "Let's not fight about this. I hate fighting. You know that."

Debra looked to be on the verge of saying something before she caught herself and reconsidered. With a merciful nod, she turned and left the room. Laura listened to her footfall on the stair runner, the occasional creak of a tread, movement along the upstairs hall, then the closing of the bathroom door. Only when she heard the sound of the shower did she turn back toward the den.

"Damn it, Jeff," she whispered, "where are you?"

Don't Miss These Enthralling Novels by Barbara Delinsky, Available from HarperCollins

Moment to Moment

From the first moment Russ Ettinger meets Dana Madison, he feels the overwhelming urge to protect her. But Dana has been protected all of her life and is determined to be loved only as a strong and independent woman.

The Carpenter's Lady

Writer Debra Barry and carpenter Graham Reid are two people seeking to forget their pasts. Debra moves to the country after her painful divorce and hires Graham to redesign her new home. But as the house comes together Debra and Graham start thinking of building a future.

A Time to Love

Arielle Pasteur flies to St. Maarten, to a villa on a private beach, looking for solitude. Instead, she finds herself sharing the hideaway with a man who gives the impression of being an overbearing, scornful egotist. Yet behind the facade lurks a gentleness that makes Arielle question whether it's solitude she really craves.

Fast Courting

Magazine writer Nia Phillips is assigned to interview the five most eligible men on the East Coast. Her article hits a snag when number five, head coach of Boston's pro basketball team, refuses to be interviewed. But the game of love has just begun.

Rekindled

Here are two Barbara Delinsky novels in one volume. *The Flip Side of Yesterday* and *Lilac Awakening* are two of her favorite romantic stories. Revised by the author and republished by HarperCollins, these stories have been rekindled.

Sweet Ember

Stephanie Wright was a nineteen-year-old camp counselor when she met and fell in love with Douglas Weston, a devastatingly handsome, older tennis instructor. Eight years later Stephanie returns to the camp where she was loved and betrayed, and the truth of that long-ago summer comes to light.

A Woman's Place

Claire Raphael is stunned when, upon her return from a hectic business trip, her husband serves her with divorce papers. He takes the house and custody of the children, too. But Claire has had to fight for every success in her life, and she's not about to give up now.

Finger Prints

Carly is the name she was given by the witness protection program. Even with a new identity, however, she is afraid her enemies will find her. Ryan Cornell is a young attorney who is fascinated by this secretive woman. But Carly cannot so easily reveal herself to another, however great the temptation.

Sensuous Burgundy

Small town assistant DA Laura Grandine and big-city lawyer Maxwell Kraig face off in an explosive courtroom battle. Yet it is the first time either has met their match for wit or will, and neither can deny the power of their attraction.

Together Alone

Emilie, Kay and Celeste have been best friends forever. When their daughters go off to college, however, each mother must find herself as a woman again. Barbara Delinsky expertly interweaves their stories in a beautiful work that is at once moving, romantic and real.

Variation on a Theme

When flutist Rachel Busek and rough-hewn private investigator Jim Guthrie meet, they quickly discover that they are the perfect complement to each other. But there are troubling pieces of her past that Rachel must uncover before she can trust herself to love Jim completely.